THE CREMATORY CAT

THE CREMATORY CAT

Karen Buck

iUniverse, Inc.

New York Lincoln Shanghai

The Crematory Cat

iUniverse, Inc.

For information address:
iUniverse, Inc.
2021 Pine Lake Road, Suite 100
Lincoln, NE 68512
www.iuniverse.com

ISBN: 0-595-28342-X (pbk)
ISBN: 0-595-74988-7 (cloth)

Printed in the United States of America

PROLOGUE

▼

The highway ran straight as a stick into the Mexico desert. Border patrol officer Bob O'Reilly sat in his air-conditioned patrol booth watching an oasis mirage shimmer in the late-afternoon heat. Much as he liked being the king of this one-man border crossing that had been established soon after the 9/11 terrorist attacks, it got damn lonely out here, and it was hot too. Every time he had to go outside he started to sweat again. He glanced at his watch. Only another hour until Howard gets here, thank God, he thought. A cold beer's gonna go down real good tonight.

A dark speck wiggled on the edge of the mirage. Good, a car. Bob was ready for damn near anything to break the monotony.

"Hey, Luis! How are ya doin'? Been down to visit the family again, huh?" Bob said, sauntering over to the car stopped at his gate.

"Hi, Bob. Yeah, you know how mothers are. If I miss a week I suffer for two." Luis Perez got out of his car and stretched. He opened the back passenger door and picked up a leash. "C'mon out, Dolly."

A fawn-colored Greyhound unfolded herself from the seat and stepped out onto the sand. She too stretched, then squatted and urinated. Bob gave the interior of the car a cursory examination. Dolly's papers were on the front seat, but she and Luis had made so many crossings here that Bob didn't give them a second glance.

"Do I pass inspection, officer?" asked Luis with a laugh.

Bob laughed and slapped Luis on the back. "Hell, you have to trust somebody in this world. Glad you had a good visit with your folks. I'll see you next week."

Bob watched Luis settle Dolly into the back seat then he lifted the gate that blocked the road. With a wave out his window, Luis drove into Arizona.

Bob went back into his cool booth with a sigh of relief. He sat down and let his eyes follow Luis' car until it was out of sight. Nice guy, he thought.

CHAPTER 1

▼

"Doreen, what are you doing?"

The aide turned to me, formula dripping on the floor from the tube she was holding.

"It's time to start this guy's feeding." She waved the tube at the unmoving figure in the bed. "I was just going to hook him up."

I clenched my teeth to keep from screaming. "Thank you anyway, Doreen, but that's not something that you should be doing. You know that."

"I don't know why not. It's not exactly a tough thing to do. Any idiot could do it."

"I know it seems like that, but there's more to it than just plugging the tube in and starting the pump," I said, picking up a large syringe to test and make sure that the tube that snaked down the patient's nose really was in his stomach where it belonged. I forced air through the tube while listening with my stethoscope. I heard gurgling, so I was fairly confident that the tube had remained in his stomach and hadn't migrated into his lungs.

"Remember what happened when that tube moved out of place into Mable Andersen's lungs and she ended up dying of aspiration pneumonia, Doreen?"

Doreen sneered at me. "Oh, you just want to be a hotshot, Maggie. This tube is always in place and this gomer never moves a muscle anyway."

"Please don't call him that. He may be unconscious, but he can hear us. Besides, we move him around all the time to change the bed and do his therapy. This tube could easily have migrated." I took the syringe off the tube while the aide stood and scowled at me. I connected the feeding tube to the patient's nasal feeding tube and started the formula flowing.

"Well, I still think that's a stupid reason and I'll do what I need to do," Doreen hissed at me.

"If I find you doing this again I'll have to talk to Martha," I told her, hoping the mention of the dragon-lady unit nurse manager would get through to her.

"Go ahead and tattle, asshole, then see how much help you get from me from now on." Doreen stomped off.

I looked at the clock with a sigh, 7:30. Thank God. The night nurse would be in any minute to relieve me. I had about had it.

After giving report on the day's activities to the nurse relieving me, I went into the locker room and flopped into a chair, exhausted. With my feet stretched out in front of me I studied my ankles, which was easy to do since my scrub pants rode halfway up my legs. Didn't the manufacturers know that some nurses are close to six feet tall?

I was almost too tired to change into my own clothes. The hospital, in their usual divine wisdom, felt that the first place to make economies was to cut the nursing staff. Now instead of being responsible for two critically ill patients each shift, I had four, with an assortment of skilled or not-so-skilled nurse aides to assist me. I didn't know why I let this bother me so much now. My resignation letter was lying on Martha's desk; she would find it in the morning, and in a few minutes I would leave this hospital forever. But, I was also beginning to think that the ICU work I loved might not be where I would continue my career after all. Besides, these ankles that looked okay today would be blown up like party balloons after a few more years of 12-hour shifts on concrete floors.

"You planning on spending the night? I thought you had two weeks off starting tonight." Pam said as she came in, ripping the snaps open on her scrub top. "I can't wait to get out of this place."

"Yeah," I sighed, "Me too. I just had to try and gather up enough energy to move. You on tomorrow?"

"No, it's my first of eight off. Joe and I are going down to Ocean Shores for a few days. We're going to leave tonight so there will be no chance of Martha calling me to come in extra. You going anywhere special?"

I bit my lip to stop the words I wanted to say. Pam had been a good work friend and I wanted to tell her that this was my last day here, but didn't. I just wasn't ready to explain everything that had gone on.

"No, not really. Your trip sounds great, though, Pam. Have a good time."

"'Bye," she said and flipped her hand in farewell as she left the locker room.

I forced myself upright and changed my clothes, then put the notes I had brought with me into Pam's mailbox and into those of a few other nurses and aides to whom I had become close. They will be pissed, I thought, that they couldn't throw me the usual good-bye party, but this is the way I have to do it.

I slipped into my sandals, thinking about Pam and her planned trip. At one time I too would have been in a hurry to get home and see my husband, but those days were gone. All I could think about now was how much I wanted to put the cats in their carriers, toss my last few belongings in the car, and hit the road. One more night, just one more night, in that elegant townhouse that now felt like a prison. How could I ever have made such a huge mistake?

CHAPTER 2

▼

"Okay, Cleo, Henry, this is it." I deflated the air mattress and rolled up my sleeping bag. Waking up came early with the sun pouring through the naked windows—even the curtains had been sold. I stood up and stretched. The Space Needle was "out" this morning, it glistened in the thin salt-water air like a king's jeweled scepter stabbed into the ground of Seattle Center. It held my gaze for a minute. That was one view I would miss.

The cats watched me work, Henry curious, Cleo anxious. She knew something was up. I would have to pick just the right moment to grab her and get her into her carrier; she thought all carrier travel was to the vet's and feared it. Henry, though, loved any sort of action. He would jump into his carrier by himself.

I took a last walk through the townhouse to make sure I had left nothing behind—that was easy, except for my bedroll and luggage, the place was empty. The pieces of furniture I had been allowed to keep were in storage, waiting for me to find a home for them. I put my toothbrush in my bag. There, I was ready.

In the living room Henry dashed away after a rolling dust bunny and Cleo stopped watching me to track him. This was my moment. I picked her up and rubbed her head and stuffed her into her carrier. Oh the wails and sobs! I knew once I got her in the car she would be struck dumb with fear, so I ignored her agonies.

Henry abandoned the dust bunny and was sitting in his carrier, ears perked and whiskers pushed forward, eager for adventure. There was no more reason to linger; I could get breakfast on the road. I locked the townhouse door for the last time, shoved the key through the mail slot, and headed for the elevators, cats and luggage on a courtesy cart.

With a whump that echoed around the underground garage, I closed the tail-gate on my new-to-me Chevy Blazer. It was a far cry from the Audi that Phil had insisted I drive, but certainly felt more like me than the fancy car had. I hopped into the driver's seat, turned on the ignition, and headed for the exit and free-dom.

I didn't know exactly where I would end up, but at least it would be better than the state penitentiary in Walla Walla, where Phil Scott, my ex-husband and convicted felon, now made his home. I hoped some big gorilla would choose Phil as his "special friend;" the jerk would deserve it.

CHAPTER 3

▼

Seattle, Washington, had been home for a few years, but my roots ran deep in Spokane. My great-great-grandparents had homesteaded on Moran Prairie back in the late 1800s and there was actually a Jackson Road still there—the one they had cut through the wilderness to their place. I had always liked the big city-small town feel there, so it seemed natural to move back after getting away from Phil Scott.

He kept me so isolated in Seattle, I thought, as I found myself transfixed by the miles of sagebrush-studded scabland in the middle of the state. The sky felt like a huge blue bowl inverted above me and the long sweep of highway across the Columbia River at the small town of Vantage was breathtaking. The first view of Spokane from the Sunset Hill with Mount Spokane's imposing height in the distance glistening with late spring snow brought a lump to my throat.

I left the freeway as soon as I was in the city. The little liquor and gift store I'd remembered was still there on Third Avenue. I went in and bought a bottle of champagne and two flutes.

Georgia Delman, a friend from high school, welcomed me into her house. "This'll be perfect," she said, taking me around to the back and opening an outside door. "Rod and I built this granny flat for his mother and even put up a kennel for her asthmatic old dog. Wouldn't you know—about the time we finished it she decided to buy a condo in Palm Springs! But now you'll be able to get some use out of it, anyway."

Georgia was one of the few people I had kept in touch with, or I should say, one of the few people Phil allowed me to keep in touch with, since my marriage and move to Seattle. When I wrote and told her what had happened, she had been delighted to be able to offer me a place to stay until I could get settled.

I set Henry and Cleo's carriers in the kennel and opened the doors. They came out and made a quick inspection then ran to the dirt and started to dig.

"This is really nice, Georgia. It's so good of you to let me stay here." I popped the champagne cork and poured some for each of us. "To the first day of the rest of my life—it's going to be great!" We clicked glasses and drank.

C H A P T E R 4

▼

The next morning I headed out to reacquaint myself with my home town. It had been awhile and things had changed. New skywalks had been added to the downtown system, connecting more buildings together. But, The Crescent was long gone and there were more empty store fronts than I remembered. The city had built a new public library with an incredible view of the Spokane River, but the gondolas in Riverfront Park that used to take tourists and residents on breath-taking trips over the river's falls hung unused on sagging cables.

I stood on the Monroe Street bridge and leaned over the rail. Water boomed past beneath my feet throwing spray into my face, hurrying its way toward the Columbia River and eventually the Pacific Ocean. The concrete was crumbling, though, and I remembered the story in the Spokesman-Review that morning discussing how the bridge would soon need to be closed for repairs.

I got back in the car and followed the river upstream east toward the region known loosely as "the valley." One of my favorite areas, I could see that the once quiet and rural valley had grown in all directions. The boarding stable, a bit of heaven where I used to visit as an equine-obsessed teen-ager, was still in business, but five acre "mini ranches" had taken over most of the riding land that surrounded it.

Leaving the mini ranches behind me, I continued east on Sprague Avenue, the main east-west thoroughfare that bisected the valley, toward the Washington-Idaho border. Sprague had grown from an occasionally-busy two lane road into a traffic-clogged, six-lane headache. I found that shopping malls, businesses, factories, and homes had sprung up clear to the border on land where apple orchards used to reign supreme.

Just before Sprague shot me onto the I-90 interstate I turned around. I needed a bathroom and coffee.

I found both at the Fred Meyer store at Sprague and Sullivan. Refreshed, I looked around at the other businesses that shared the parking lot. Kinkos, a 50% Off Card Shop, and what was this? Factory 2-U? I had always been a bargain hunter and this sounded intriguing. I went in.

Jeans and tailored shorts in the summer were as casual as Phil had ever wanted me to be. He felt I had an image to maintain, even at home. What a load of crap, I thought, I'm a sweats gal. I piled a shopping basket high with sweat pants and shirts. Only $2 a piece, this was fabulous. I added stacks of kitchen, bath, hand towels, and wash clothes in a rainbow of delicious hues. I would use them until they were so thin I could see through them, then cut them up for rags. Phil had only wanted white in our silver and white bathrooms and in the white, white, white, kitchen, and would toss a towel the minute it showed any sign of wear. I found a rug I loved for in front of a sink I didn't even have yet. This was a great place. I had dreaded the expense of replacing all my linen, but these prices were such a relief. I had tossed all that Phil and I had shared into a Goodwill bag. It was all good stuff, but I knew I would never be able to bear to have it touch my skin again.

I had bought the bed for the townhouse, but sold it before leaving Seattle. Something else I couldn't stand to use again. I would come back here for sheets when I needed them. I stuffed my haul into the Blazer and continued my voyage of re-discovery.

Coming back toward town, I turned north on Argonne Road, one of the few ways to get across the Spokane River from the south to the north part of the valley. Argonne had finally made the plunge beneath the Burlington Northern Railroad tracks at the Trent intersection. This was one of the best changes I had seen today. How well I recalled the time spent waiting for freight trains that seemed endless to get across Argonne. With the underpass in place, the volume of traffic using Argonne and going through the tiny town of Millwood increased substantially. I remembered when Argonne was two lanes wide and sidewalk-less. It now four-laned its way from Sprague to Bigelow-Gulch Road, which connected the valley to the north side of the city.

The Argonne bridge was slated for replacement and it would soon be off-limits to the boy scrambling up to stand on the railing, his skin goose-bumped. It was not really swimming weather yet, the river would be bone-chilling cold, but I knew he would have to jump, his girlfriend was watching. I saw him make the leap from the bridge into the water below that his predecessors had been making for generations. It felt good to be back.

I went back to Georgia's house and sat staring at the phone. There was still one call I had to make, and I dreaded it.

CHAPTER 5

▼

"Hi, Mom? It's Maggie," I said to her voice mail. "I'm sorry to have missed you." What a lie that was. I would be able to bring her up to date on things and she could have her initial tantrum before I actually had to talk to her.

"I wanted to let you know that Phil did end up being convicted and sent to prison. After the divorce was final, I decided to move back to Spokane and I'll let you know my address and phone number as soon as I know what they are."

I hung up the phone and my sigh of relief had the kitchen curtains swaying. My mother. I had spent my whole life trying to live up to her expectations. She was so thrilled with my marriage to Phil, he was, after all, a corporate hot shot and she could brag to her friends about him.

To her, image is everything. I once had her almost knock me down on a Spokane sidewalk when she saw one of the upper management executives from the insurance company where she worked passing us going the other way. She had thrown herself in front of him and given him a big hello.

He had nodded and smiled, but I expected him to duck into a nearby store to change his underwear. She had about startled him out of his shoes.

"Who was that?" I had asked.

"That's Roy Traber, he's the vice president of the company. I can' t stand the man—he thinks he's the wart on the ass of creation," she said, tossing her head as she delivered what was her favorite condemnation of someone she thought was snooty or arrogant.

"So why'd you break your neck to say hi to him, then?" I wanted to know.

"Oh, I had to. What would people think if they saw us pass on the sidewalk and me not speak to him?" she said and waved gaily at Roy as he walked on.

"But you had to practically knock me and fifteen other people down to get to him; he was nowhere near us. How would anybody even have noticed?"

She looked pityingly at me. I just didn't get it, that was obvious. She started one of her lectures about maintaining appearances and I tuned her out. Just like I had been doing since I was six years old and heard the first one.

The divorce from Phil was going to drive her crazy. Even though she had moved back to her hometown of San Diego, where there were are 'my kind of people who know how to live a proper life,' she still felt every misstep I took was a direct slap at her and what "people" would think of her, for having such a failure of a daughter.

Beth, my younger sister, was smarter. Even though mom thought she could do absolutely nothing wrong, ever, she still found a need to escape. Beth had met and married an Irishman and he had taken her to Ireland to live, where she had an adorable Irish cottage out in the country and had obligingly presented mom with the required 2.4 grandchildren. But Beth had run away after all, I thought, so I guess cloying over-attention was as bad as constant criticism.

I, on the other hand, seemed to do nothing right. Even though mom saw Phil as the catch of the century and she loved bragging to her friends about our downtown home and the views of the Space Needle and Mt. Rainier, she wished he worked for a more-prestigious company, somehow home improvement products just were not fancy enough. And she still was not sure if she approved of my being a nurse, either.

"I don't understand why you have to work on weekends and holidays," she would often say, her tone just shy of an out-and-out whine.

I would answer, like I did every time we had the conversation, that people were still sick in the hospital on weekends and holidays and needed to be taken care of.

"It just seems that somebody else could do it," was her stock reply. I tried to explain how I did not work all weekends or all holidays, that the staff took turns, but she didn't hear it. All she knew was that she would have to admit to one of her pals that I was not present for some important occasion. After a couple of years of struggling to explain, I stopped. I just told if I would be in attendance or not and let her fuss.

But, at least she could brag about my address and Phil's title. I had dreaded telling her about his crimes and my filing for divorce and the conversation had met all my expectations.

"Why, you have to stand behind him," she had said, indignant.

I had to shake my head to try and clear out the cobwebs that she spun there. "But, Mother, he stole from the company, he threatened me, and he actually had some creep physically assault me when he didn't get his own way, not to mention the fact that he was cheating on me, too. I can't imagine why you would want me to stay with someone like that. He talked about killing me, for God's sake."

"Well," she hmmphed, "I still wish you wouldn't end up with a divorce on your record so soon."

Record? What record? Is there someone with a big ledger keeping track? Am I going to have to wear a big red D on my forehead?

I tried again. "Aren't you always worrying about my safety?"

Now she really sounded indignant. "Of course I am. It's just…"

"Never mind, Mom." I could hear the 'what will people think?' in her voice. "It's late and I'm tired. I'll let you know what I plan on doing. Good night."

As I pulled the phone away from my ear I heard her pleading voice, "Just think about it," she said.

Well, now she knew my decision. I could anticipate a bawling out when she finally got a chance to talk to me, but at least I was spared dealing with the initial hysteria my news would create.

CHAPTER 6

▼

Georgia came in just as I was hanging up the phone.

"Your mom?"

"You could tell just by looking at me, huh? Yeah, but I got lucky. She wasn't home and I just left her a message. Even with all the stuff that went on, she still doesn't think I should have divorced Phil. I've never really told you what happened—want to hear the story?"

"Let me get some coffee going." Georgia went to the sink and turned on the water. She poured it into the coffee maker and put coffee grounds in the filter. Mr. Coffee started to drip and she sat down across from me. "Okay, tell me."

"Well, you remember how Phil and I met just as I finished nursing school? I thought he was Mr. Wonderful. Kind, loving, understanding, supportive, the whole package. I really thought I had struck the Mother Lode. But, a couple of years after the wedding, he started to get weird, began to drink a lot, and became very secretive. He had never really told me how much money he made, just said that it was enough to support us, so I put my salary in a couple of IRAs and into CDs. I wrote you about the townhouse and the fancy cars, remember?"

"Sounded like heaven," said Georgia, nodding.

"At first it was. But, one day I found a bunch of bills that were overdue, some on accounts I didn't even know we had. Then, I found a foreclosure notice nailed on the front door of the townhouse. That was a real shocker. But, when I asked Phil about all this stuff he just exploded, telling me it was somehow my fault. He demanded that I liquidate all the investments I had made and give the money to him the very next day. Then, he actually slapped and threatened me."

"Oh, my God, I had no idea, Maggie! What did you do?"

"I tried to leave, but he told me that he would hunt me down. Then, he bragged about having an affair with one of the nurse aides at the hospital, accused me of stealing and selling drugs, fooling around with the patients and doctors, it just went on and on. Finally he slammed out of the house, telling me to have the money the next day and that he would be back, with help. Then I really was scared. I called the cops."

"Good for you. Did they listen to you?"

"Yes. They actually came out and put voice-activated tape recorders in the house and then waited with me the next day for Phil to come back."

"…and he did come back?"

"Oh, Georgia, it was awful." I could feel the tears start. I let them flow. "He called me a whore and a cunt. I had gotten some money together, but of course you can't just get the money instantly out of IRAs or CDs. He told me I was holding out on him, then he and this big oaf that came with him, Norm, a sloppy fat guy with awful, broken, yellow teeth, grabbed me and tried to rape me. The cops jumped out from where they were hiding just in time to stop them." I laughed shakily and dried my eyes, "It was quite a scene."

Georgia got up and fumbled for coffee cups, her hands trembling. "I hardly know what to say. He could have killed you."

"Yup, and there's more. The next morning I called off work, boy did that ever make the nurse manager mad. I was trying to figure out what to do next when a detective came to the house looking for Phil. For a minute I was afraid he was out of jail already, but it turned out that the Seattle police's fraud division had been watching him for some time. Turned out he had sucked a bunch of money out of Home Improvement, Inc.'s books over the last year or two."

Georgia and I sipped coffee for a quiet minute.

"What happened to Phil, anyway?" she asked. "He seemed like such a great guy."

"I don't know. I suppose I must not have known him as well as I thought I did. There was some talk of gambling, and he did buy lots of fancy stuff for the house. A safety deposit box was found, but it had only a few hundred dollars in it. They said there were a couple of million dollars that couldn't be accounted for and they never did find it. He probably has it squirreled away somewhere."

"He's in jail, I presume." Georgia's eyes flashed fury.

"Yes, for at least ten years." I got up to refill my cup. "That's not really the worst of it, though."

"More? There's *more*?"

"Yes, just before my whole life blew up in my face I discovered I was pregnant." I saw Georgia's eyes drop to my stomach, where no evidence of a baby on the way showed.

"No, I'm not pregnant anymore. When Phil and his hired help attacked me, one of them punched me in the stomach, hard enough to cause a miscarriage. In a way I'm glad, I wouldn't want to have a child that was part Phil, but it also broke my heart. I had been pregnant just long enough for the baby to seem real."

Georgia got up and threw her arms around me. "Oh, Maggie," she sobbed, "I wish I had known; I wish there was something I could have done."

For a moment we hugged and wept. "I wish things had turned out differently too," I whispered.

That night I lay in the bed in Georgia's granny flat, feeling pounds lighter. Cleo was curled at my feet and Henry snuggled against my back. For the first time in months, I slept all night.

CHAPTER 7

▼

I didn't want to impose on Georgia and Rod for too long, so the next morning I started to house-shop. I knew what I wanted, a ranch style house with maybe a little land around it. I hoped to get out from the city; I wanted some space and peace and quite after the years of living in downtown Seattle.

Over the next couple of weeks my Realtor, Brian Anderson, showed me several places. I didn't have to worry about qualifying for a loan, the townhouse had sold for a bundle, so I knew I would have a big down payment, but it just didn't seem like I could find that ideal house. I knew Brian was getting a little frustrated with me, but I couldn't help it.

Then he called and said he had a very unusual listing to show me.

"Are you still interested in living out in the country?" he asked.

"Yes, as long as it isn't too far out or too expensive," I told him.

"Well, okay. I have something unique to show you that's in your price range. I'll be there in fifteen minutes and we will go see it."

Georgia's house was near downtown, but just twenty minutes after picking me up, Brian pulled into a driveway in the foothills of Mouth Spokane. A wonderful driveway that crossed a plank bridge with slender skinned logs making up the side railings. A small stream cascaded under the bridge from uphill, the water that unique milky blue color that was fresh snow melt. I was already in love with the house and I hadn't even seen it yet. As we went over the little bridge Brian said, "Okay, here's the deal with this place. All I can show you today is the outside. Then, if you think you are interested, I have an application for you to fill out before you can go in and check out the interior, that is, if your application is accepted."

"What are you talking about?" I asked him. "Application?"

"Yeah. This seller, her name is Eleanor Branson, is a bit different. She wants to make sure that just the right person buys her house, so here's the deal. If your application is approved, you get to go in and look around. The application is actually just a letter you write telling her what you like about the place, any changes you might anticipate making, and why you want to buy this house. Then, if your letter is chosen and you see the inside and like it, you get the opportunity to buy it. Her price is not negotiable, but quite reasonable, and, like I said earlier, within your price range." We came around the bend in the driveway and I got my first look at the house.

I had seen so many new houses with the huge garage out in front wagging the little dog of a house in the back. This place had a huge garage too, but of a different sort.

"Odd, isn't it?" said Brian.

"It is different, but I like it." An old orange pickup glowered from the shed off the right side of the house and I could see a snow plow leaning against the back wall. "Does the truck stay?"

"Yes. Eleanor calls it Herman," Brian said. "It's something you'll need to use to plow your driveway if the snow gets deep."

I got out to look around. The main house was log, with dark green trim. The roof was steeply clad in dark green aluminum, smart here where the snow could stack up. At the right side of the house next to the garage housing the pickup was the huge garage, more of a shop building really, built of metal, but a dark honey-gold brown that seemed to melt into the hill behind it. There was a car-width door in the front, as well as a standard door. But, it did not appear this was intended for cars, for there was a single car garage on the other end of the house and there was no real driveway leading up to the shop. Two ancient maple trees spread their limbs over the roof an each side of the house's front door. I could see what looked like a skylight on the roof, too.

In back the yard was not huge, but certainly large enough for the dog I wanted to have some day. There was a large kennel with a dog door built into the house wall. That would be perfect for the cats, they could go outside and still be safe. I looked up and saw a red-tailed hawk riding a thermal high above us. A cat would make a nice snack for him and there were coyotes around too, I bet. I was glad the dog kennel was built from sturdy chain link fencing and had a top of chain link on it as well.

The yard was fenced with chain link fencing too, it looked like it was about eight feet tall with three rows of barbed wire on the top. I'll put a dog door into the door to the house, I thought, then maybe make the other door into the kennel a little smaller for the cats. But, don't go putting the cart before the horse. You don't even know if you are going to be allowed to see the inside of this house yet!

I looked out into the yard. In one corner was a huge old apple tree, bursting with blossoms, and in the another corner stood a horse chestnut tree, also in bloom. A row of smaller trees and bushes ran along the back fence, almost making the chain link invisible.

"The fence was built to keep the deer out of the yard," Brian told me.

I nodded, it made good sense if I wanted to use what appeared to be a vegetable garden area cleared off in one corner. I was glad to see the apple and chestnut trees had branches that were on the outside of the fence too; I would be able to share their bounty with the local wildlife.

Sliding glass doors on the back of the house led to a deck. A four-person hot tub sat in one corner and there was a rolled metal awning that could be opened out over the deck. The doors were curtained, as were all the windows. I could not see into the house from anywhere.

"It's actually a four bedroom, two bathroom house," Brian said. "I know it doesn't look very big from the outside, but you'd be amazed. There's no basement, except for a utility room that contains the furnace and the water heater and some shelves for storage, but there is lots of storage space inside, as well as an attic. What do you think?"

"I love it," I told him. "Where's this application I need to fill out?"

CHAPTER 8

▼

Back at Georgia's I sat down at her kitchen table. Like Brian had said, the application really only asked for my name, the rest was to be a letter of introduction of me, why I wanted this house, and what my ideal house would be. I booted up my laptop computer and opened Microsoft WORD. This could be fun.

Dear Eleanor Branson:

Hello, my name is Maggie Jackson. I am a Registered Nurse and a professional quilter, although I haven't had time to do much quilting for awhile. I was born and raised in Spokane, but spent the last few years in Seattle. I had been married to a man who ended up being an embezzler and actually assaulted me. It's a long sad story that I won't bore you with right now.

I am so glad to be back in Spokane and was thrilled to be able to at least see the outside of your house. I like the location, and have always wanted a house with a creek running by it. Plus, the big shop would be ideal. But more on that later.

You want to know what my ideal house would be? Okay, here goes. At least three bedrooms, one for me, one for an office, and one for guests, or who knows? maybe a child some day. I want a kitchen that is big enough to work comfortably in, as I love to cook, but nothing fancy. It would be nice to have a breakfast nook or space for a small table and a couple of chairs. I would like a separate, more formal, dining area too, where there could be a larger table. Two bathrooms would be perfect, but I could manage with one.

The house would be all on one level and the washer and dryer would be close to the bedrooms and bathrooms, where the dirty clothes are generated. A mudroom with an entrance from the outside would be perfect.

I prefer forced air heating and would like to have air conditioning for the summer. I would love a fireplace too.

Now, about the shop. Like I said, I am a professional quilter and have what is called a long arm quilting machine. This is a sewing machine that sits on tracks that run along the front and back edges of a long, narrow table; my machine is a Noltings and its table is fourteen feet long, so the shop would make an ideal quilting workroom. There would be more than enough room for my sewing machines and the long arm machine. It would also be fun to be able to teach small quilting classes and I bet that shop would be big enough for a large table or two where I could do that. So, even though I don't include that as something that would go with my ideal house, seeing it makes it so.

I hope I get a chance to tour your house. I already love it from the outside.

Sincerely yours,

Maggie Jackson

I signed the letter and addressed it to Mrs. Branson. Now all I could do was wait.

CHAPTER 9

▼

I told Georgia about the house the next morning over breakfast.

"I think I've found the house I want. But, I have to be approved by the buyer before I can even try to buy it. I had hoped to get out of your hair pretty soon, but if this deal doesn't go through I'll have to start all over."

"You have to be approved by the buyer? What's that all about?"

"Brian told me that Eleanor Branson, the owner of the house, isn't really looking to make a bunch of money off the sale of her place. The insurance policy that her husband had taken out back in the 1950s paid off handsomely and she just wants to sell it for what it cost them. I guess Mrs. Branson is picky about who lives in her house, though."

"Huh, that's sort of different, isn't it? Well, don't worry about it a bit," she said. "Stay here as long as you need to. That granny flat we had put in for Rod's mother is ideal for you with its separate entrance and kennel for the cats. Besides, you know we're leaving in a couple of weeks to stay for a month at that cabin where we own a time share. I'll be glad to have you here to keep an eye on things. I won't have to go through the hassle of stopping the mail and the paper and everything. That is if you wouldn't mind..."

"Good heavens, no!" I said, "The least I can do if you're letting me stay here is put your mail and paper in while you're gone."

"Oh, good," she said. "Then let's just wait and see what happens with this house you looked at, okay?"

CHAPTER 10

▼

Two days passed in agonizing slowness. Never had a silent phone seemed so mocking—I was sure it knew how much I wanted it to ring. I caught myself checking for a dial tone, making sure the phone was still in service. When it finally rang, and Georgia said it was for me, it seemed to take me an hour to get to the phone table and pick up the receiver.

"Hey, Maggie, good news!" said Brian, sounding excited. "Mrs. Branson liked your intro letter and she said you can take a look at the inside of the house. Can I come pick you up right now?"

As Brian pulled into the driveway over the little bridge I was again struck by the perfect location and look of the house. I could hardly wait to get inside.

Once inside the front door I had to laugh.

"What's funny?" said Brian.

"Oh, Brian, this is so amazing. In my letter to Eleanor Branson describing my perfect house you would think I was sitting in here to write it. This is exactly what my dream house would look like."

We went through the rest of the house. Like Brian had said, it was small-looking from the outside, but the interior was spacious. The Branson's had chosen a lush forest green carpet for the living room and dining floors then continued the same carpeting into the bedrooms. There were four generous-sized bedrooms with the master even bigger than the other three, two baths, one attached to the master bedroom with a Jacuzzi tub and a large separate shower, enclosed in pebbly frosted glass. There was a breakfast nook in the kitchen, and a mudroom with a door into the back yard between the bedroom wing and the kitchen. Not only were the washer and dryer there, a stall shower snuggled in one corner as well.

The dog door that led outside to the big kennel was the mudroom too, in the back wall of the house. Brian showed me where a switch was that activated the stairs that led to the attic. He flicked it and the stairs lowered down from the ceiling. No need to tug on a rope.

A side door led into the shop space. It was nice to know there was a way in there from the house without having to go outside.

"Here's another interesting feature," Brian said, leading me into the kitchen. He opened the large pantry door next to the refrigerator. He lifted up a nearly invisible flap of wood on a side wall and flipped a switch.

The entire interior shelving section of the pantry began to move forward into the kitchen, almost like it was being carried by a forklift. Behind the shelves was a door.

"This door leads into the shop. Then there is a hidden door in the side wall of the shop, too, as well as one that opens out the back wall of the shop into the back yard outside of the fence. The Bransons were a little paranoid and installed this as an escape route if someone should break into the house."

"How amazing," I said.

"Yes, and did you notice that this mechanism is completely silent, and that they located it so that you can't see it from anywhere except right here where we're standing in the kitchen?"

"No. I hadn't noticed that, but I see what you mean, Brian. I can't see into the dining room from here like you can from the other side of the kitchen. I guess this is a good idea, but it just seems too strange."

"I suppose you could disconnect the wires…"

"No," I said, "I'd leave it. You never know when something like this might come in handy."

We went through the door. It was a bit spooky, after Brian closed the pantry door behind us there were a few seconds of total darkness until an overhead light came on. We were in a shelf-lined, closet-like space with just enough room for the two of us to stand without crowding each other. As Brian pushed open the door to the shop the light went off and like he had said, we found ourselves in the shop, which was just a big empty space. The walls had been paneled in knotty pine with storage cabinets all along one side. The floor was wood, sanded baby-bottom smooth and probably coated with polyurethane, from the glossy look of it. A pot-bellied stove that burned gas snuggled in one corner. I could picture a small rug and a couple of cozy chairs placed on either side of it.

The two hidden doors, both the one from the house and the one leading to the outside in the back wall of the shop Brian had told me about, were visible only if you knew where to look for them. The handles looked like shelves, with a catch on the under side of the shelf, and could not be seen unless you were down on the floor looking up. I glanced around the big space again. This would make a perfect sewing and quilting room.

"Well, Maggie, what do you think?"

"I love it, Brian. Please tell the Mrs. Branson I would like to be considered as the future owner of her house."

CHAPTER 11

▼

The next morning I had just sat down to breakfast when the phone rang. It was Brian.

"The house is yours, Maggie!"

I was flabbergasted. "You are kidding. She choose me?"

Brian laughed. "I wasn't allowed to tell you before, but Eleanor had said that after she read your application letter she didn't even look at any of the others again. She said all you needed to do was be as pleased with the inside as you had been with the outside and the place was yours. I think the key part was that Eleanor is a quilter too. She is delighted that you are going to turn the shop into a quilting studio."

"This is so amazing. What's next?"

"Well, there will be some papers to sign, all the usual formalities. Eleanor Branson is going to carry the contract though, so there's no financial stuff to worry about. She is giving you a better interest rate than any bank or mortgage company could, too. She said you can start moving in today, if you like. I'll drop the keys off within the hour, okay?"

"Okay," I whispered, "I'll be here."

I dropped the phone into its cradle. Henry was sitting on the kitchen table, gazing at me with soft yellow eyes.

"Oh, Henry," I said, "We have a house." Then all I could do was drop my head onto my crossed arms and weep. It had been so long since things had gone well for me. I hoped this was the beginning of a happier life.

By the time Georgia and Rod were back from their vacation I was ready to move myself and the cats and unpack the last of the boxes. My furniture and quilting machine had arrived by truck and had been installed in the house and the shop. Now all that was left were those formalities Brian had mentioned.

What a pleasure it had been to sign "Maggie Jackson" to the loan papers. I no longer had any further connection to Phil Scott. He was a good as dead, as far as I was concerned.

That had been mid August. Now the leaves were just starting to change color.

CHAPTER 12

▼

"Well, Henry, what do you think? Is it home now?"

Henry and Cleo were bookends on the mantle, front paws tucked neatly under their chests. Henry bobbed his head and said, "meow." He shook his head to dislodge the cobwebs hanging in his whiskers and stood up to stretch.

Slick and jet-black, Henry was, by self-coronation, alpha cat of the new house. He had led the way into every dark nook and cranny with fluffy and timid little Cleo following behind him, her belly to the ground and eyes dilated with fear. Henry had made sure that every square inch of the house had been thoroughly nosed. He went down the funny little flight of service stairs that led to the utility room and snuck up on the furnace/air conditioner to make sure the monster inside making all the noise was harmless. He hopped into the laundry tub, leaving Cleo sitting on the floor bleating with anxiety, then he went into the bathrooms and he peeked into every toilet. He marched on imperiously tall legs in and out the dog door to the outside enclosed run like he had been doing it every day of his life. Cleo watched Henry make several trips before she oozed her way out. She had a hard time getting the big dog door open, her six pounds just didn't provide the same push that Henry's seventeen did. I would have to change that dog door to a cat door for her. When I got a dog I would put the dog door into the house's back door that led to the yard.

At first glance Cleo was as black as Henry, but outside in the sunshine her coat was revealed as a rich semi-sweet chocolate brown, with black legs. I watched her sneak her way outside again, puffy brown pantaloons over her black-stockinged hind legs. I wished my rear end view were as adorable as hers.

Once back inside she was full of chatter about all the things she had smelled, seen, and heard. Henry came back in, too, squinting his pleasure at his new world.

They found their food dishes and litter box. Replete with tuna, they were now content to sit on the mantle and supervise me while I finished putting our home together.

I still needed to shop for a bed and the master bedroom was more than big enough for a queen sized bed. Phil and I had had a king size that I had gotten rid of, so I would get a queen size for me. For now I could just sleep on the sofa bed in the living room.

My Registered Nurse license hung in its frame over my desk in the bedroom I designated as my office. Like the rest of my world, the nursing board knew me as Maggie Jackson now. I was born Margaret Lynne, but my parents had always called me Lynne. The trouble was, the name seemed to me to be for a pretty little girl in fluffy dresses and I was more the jeans and T-shirt sort. As soon as I left home for college I started calling myself Maggie. My sister, who ended up with Elizabeth Anne, went by Beth. That better suited her blond curls and sweet disposition, like Maggie fit my dark hair and restless nature.

I discovered dual phone jacks in all the rooms, even the kitchen. The Qwest guy gave me a glimpse into the outside box and showed me places where four separate lines could come into the house. I could see where two of them were already wired in. Good. I would use one for the main phone and the other for the quilt shop and computer. It only took a few minutes for both lines to become operational.

I went into the living room and looked up at the cathedral ceiling. I loved the skylight there, like the one in the master bedroom. I could see gold-trimmed green leaves against the black limbs of the big maple tree and scraps of the sunset, airbrushed in flaming orange across the sky. I was also glad that the Bransons had left as many trees as possible in place. Beside with the native firs, maples, and aspen, there were volunteer apple and cherry trees along the back fence in between the ancient apple and chestnut trees at the corners.

I called Georgia and gave her my new phone number, then walked through the house—again marveling at my luck. In the mud room I stood and pondered the slate floor. In the middle was a large rectangle that had been edged with narrow strips of metal. "I wonder why they put this metal trim into the stone," I asked Henry, who had no reply. "It looks okay with the gray stone, but why go to this effort in a mud room?" I thought about it for a few seconds then shrugged and went back through the kitchen and into the living room. Decorating that room would be a challenge. The fireplace took up one wall, the one opposite had French doors to the dining room, the front wall was all windows and doors, and the north wall was taken up by built-in bookcases, shelves, and cupboards. This will have to be where the TV and stereo would go, there really is no other place available in this room. Putting the couch in the middle of the room in front of the fireplace might work. I wasn't really an interior decorator by any stretch of the imagination—I would just have to shove things around until I liked the way they looked. For now I would just leave everything huddled at one end.

I heard the refrigerator come on in the kitchen. Its hum sounded reproachful, it was not doing its job, sitting there empty. I went out and climbed into the Blazer. Time to get some groceries.

Three hours later I drove across my creek, half expecting the bridge to buckle under the loaded Blazer.

I had gotten all the necessities, food that was frozen, fresh, boxed, instant, and canned, sugar, flour, salt, and all those nonfood items, like Kleenex, toilet paper, paper towels, aluminum foil, wax paper, the works. My checkbook was still too hot to touch. And I got all the other staples of course, cat food, litter, a couple of bird feeders, bird seed, sunflower seeds, and peanuts for the squirrels and chipmunks I had already seen bouncing around outside. The birdbath wouldn't fit in the Blazer; I would have to go back for that another day.

The phone rang as I staggered in with the last bag. I picked it up.

"Hello, is this Maggie Jackson?" said an unfamiliar woman's voice. I nearly hung up, this sounded like a telemarketer and I never talked to them. But, before I could answer, she said, "This is Eleanor Branson. I charmed your friend Georgia out of your phone number. I hope it was okay she gave it to me."

"Oh, hi, Mrs. Branson, sure that was fine. I've never actually talked to you before."

She chuckled. "I did manage to sell you my house without actually meeting you, didn't I? You must have thought I was crazy."

I had to laugh with her, "Well, I did wonder."

"Larry and I had been married for almost 50 years when he suddenly took sick and died. I pretty much moved out of the house the next day. He had built it as his dream house, with a lot of input from me, of course, and I just could not stay there, it was breaking my heart, but I also just couldn't make myself deal with selling it. I just let Brian handle everything. Larry and I had a winter place we rented in Arizona and I got an opportunity to buy it, so I did. I'm just in town for a few days visiting friends."

"I am so sorry to hear about your husband, Mrs. Branson. But, I am also so thrilled with this house. You two did a wonderful job on it."

"Please call me Eleanor," she said. "Yes, it was a great house and home for our family. But, there is more to it than you know yet, even my Realtor didn't have all the details. Are you using a cordless phone?"

"Yes, I am, why?"

"Well, Larry is going to take you on a tour of the basement; the part of the house you haven't seen yet."

"I've been in the furnace room, that basement?"

"No, not just that. There's lots more. But, I'll let Larry tell you about it."

Now I was really beginning to doubt Eleanor's sanity. Larry was dead and buried, she told me so. Yet he was going to take me on a tour of the house? Eleanor must have read my thoughts, her rich chuckle came through the phone again.

"Go and open the secret escape door in the kitchen that goes to the shop. Brian showed you that, didn't he?"

"Yes, he did. Okay, here I go."

I had no trouble finding the hidden switch and the pantry again slid silently into the kitchen.

"It's open," I said.

"Good. Now, Maggie, reach way up into the back corner of the highest shelf, I think it's on the left side. You should find a small leather pouch."

I was just tall enough to reach up on the top shelf. I fumbled around and found the pouch. I pulled it down along with a shower of dust. I brushed it off and tugged open the zipper. A small tape recorder slid out into my hand.

"Okay, Eleanor, I found it; it's a tape recorder?"

"Yes. Now, I am sure the batteries in it are dead by now, but get some new ones and listen to the tape that is inside. I'm not trying to be mysterious; the tape will explain everything."

"I think I have some batteries. I'll listen to this right away."

"I'm going to say good-bye now, Maggie." Eleanor said, her voice clogging with tears, "It is still so hard for me to talk about Larry…" her voice faded away.

"Thank you for telling me about this, Eleanor. If you ever want to come visit when you are in town you are always welcome. Good-bye."

"Good-bye, Maggie," was the faint reply.

I hung up the phone and stood looking at the recorder in my hand. Now what?

CHAPTER 13

▼

There were batteries in the kitchen drawer I had chosen as the one that holds all the debris of daily life that I can never find a good place for. I put them in the recorder and pushed the play button.

After a few scratchy noises a male voice said, "Hello. This is Larry Branson. If you are listening to this tape then I am dead and you are the new owner of the house my wife and I built. I have some special things to show you. Are you in the living room now? If not, go there and go over to the built-in unit on the north wall. This is where the tour begins. Take a look at the bottom shelf in the floor to ceiling bookcase part. Run your fingers along the front edge. Feel that little button? Push it."

Like with the kitchen pantry, a push of a button caused the bookcase to move forward into the room on a silent mechanism. Behind it was a large open space.

"The bookcase should have moved open. Go into that space and flick the switch on the back wall."

There was just room for me to squeeze behind the bookcase and flip the switch on. The shelves moved shut behind me and I had a moment of claustrophobia before a faint light came on and, again without a sound, a panel in the floor slid open, revealing a set of stairs.

"Go ahead and go down," said Larry.

The stairs descended into darkness. With my toe I felt for the first step. As I let my weight down, a dim light came on at the bottom of the steps, illuminating the way. I continued down, my heart racing. What *was* this?

"Now, don't be scared," Larry said, "As you reach the bottom step the panel will slide shut above you. But, see that switch there on the wall at the bottom of the stairs? That will open the panel and move the bookcase out again. Besides, this area connects down kind of a narrow passageway to the utility room where the furnace is and you can always get out that way. It's that narrow door to your left. See it?"

"Larry, what is this?" I asked as I opened the door and looked down a short hall that ran to my left. There was a faint glow of light at the end. I turned and looked into a large room on the right with a hall extending from the back wall. Doors opened off the hall.

It was like he expected my question. "Well, in the 1950s they would have called it a bomb shelter, but I just felt the need to have a truly secure place with an escape route to the outside. The house was already built, but the basement was just an empty space. After I read a magazine story about a man back east that built a safe haven for his family I knew I had to do this. I decided to take it a step further, though, quite a few steps further, as you will see. Take a few minutes to explore."

I think you are crazy, is what I think. I turned off the recorder and looked around. This was like an apartment, living room and kitchen as one big room, just separated by a counter. Two bedrooms, and a bathroom opened off the hall, and all the rooms were furnished. Nothing was fancy, just good sturdy furniture and brand name appliances. The stove, refrigerator, and dishwasher were not as large as the ones upstairs, but would certainly be adequate. The pantry was empty and I suppose it would be a good idea to put some non-perishables down here.

There were linens in a closet outside the bathroom and bedrooms. There were no windows to the outside, but clever lighting fixtures dispelled the dungeon feeling that such a place could have had. Very nice, but weird. I had seen the Jodie Foster film, "The Panic Room," but this was way beyond what that had been. This was more like The Panic Apartment.

I clicked the recorder back on. "Okay, now that you've looked around," Larry's voice said, "I want to show you how to get out of there without going back up into the house. Go into the smaller of the bedrooms. Go into the closet and feel along the door molding by the top hinge, you should find a button, push it."

The button was there, and a push caused the wall to my left to slide away, like a pocket door. I found myself staring into the utility room at the furnace and water heater. I could see into the back yard through the sliding glass doors in this daylight basement room that I had already explored from the other side.

"Now, a couple more things. If you go out of the basement rooms through the utility room, you will need to close the door behind you. There's a switch on the wall behind the water heater for that. Also, you can go out another way. There's a closet in the living room with the same sort of switch as in the bedroom closet, but that will open up a stairway into the shop. That one will close behind you by itself when you step up to the floor of the shop and your weight comes off the top step. The switch plate by the door that goes into the main house lifts up and there's a button to open that escape hatch into the basement from the shop, too." I stopped the tape and went to look.

He was right, it did. I didn't go clear up into the shop; I would try that out after the tape was finished. I went back to the narrow door that led to the passage-way Larry had mentioned; the one that connected to the hall outside the stairway down from the bookcase and ran to the downstairs utility room. That hall really gave me the willies, it was almost like a tunnel with just an entry and exit at each end. But, it would offer a quicker escape than going into the bedroom and hunting for the switch, that was for sure. This place was like a rabbit warren. I was glad to have a guide on this first trip. I turned the recorder back on.

"Your Realtor showed you how to open the attic door with the switch in the mud room, didn't he? Well, there's one more switch in there, recessed into the wall just behind the top of the dryer that will open a panel in the floor. That leads to a rather steep staircase that's more like a ladder. That is one more way to get into the basement. You might want to pick up a phone for the basement, too. The jacks are there already and it is a separate line from the phone line upstairs. It's actually split off the extra line upstairs I had put in for a computer modem. You just need to call the phone company and get it activated. I assume the little cost for that extra line is something you won't mind."

"One step of ahead of you, there, Larry. I already did that. So that explains the metal trim in the stone floor in the mud room," I muttered, stopping the recorder. "Whew, Larry, you sure are right. I got a whole lot more house than I first knew about." I clicked the tape on again.

"One last thing," he said, "I also installed a security system that is activated from the basement. If you look in the bathroom, you will see a button in the back of the cabinet over the sink. If you push that, Sonitrol is alerted to send the police your way and also hidden cameras in the house and outside will start to tape any activity. That is being paid for out of your house payment, by the way."

I felt the hair on the back of my neck stand up and I had to sit down. This was really out there and I wasn't sure if I were glad or uncomfortable with the thought of cameras.

It was like Larry read my mind again. "Now don't sweat the cameras. They can only be activated if you push that button, and they aren't in any of the bedrooms or bathrooms, just the main living areas of the house and outside on the perimeter. There's a small TV that is also a monitor in the bigger of the bedrooms that will let you see just what the cameras are seeing, the panel that lets you choose which camera picture to watch is under the TV monitor, which has a built-in VCR so you can tape what the cameras see. Oh, and one last thing. I don't know if you found the generator in the little lean-to at the back of the shop. If the power ever goes out just start 'er up and you'll be fine until the power company fixes whatever went wrong. It burns diesel. You might want to call and get the tank drained and filled with fresh fuel though, it's probably been there a few years, by now."

Larry then told me to get a notepad and he listed the names of the people who had helped him build his fortress, along with their phone numbers should I ever need any repair work done. By the time the tape was finished tears were running down my face. I was missing this man I had never met. What a great guy he must have been to think so much about his family's safety. I couldn't imagine ever being so much in harm's way I would have to flee down here, but I was glad to have the option. This would take some getting used to, though.

I stepped back into the bedroom and wondered, if I push that closet button again will the wall close? It did. I wound my way back to the stairs I had first come down and went past them into what was set up as a living room, with couches, chairs, and end tables.

I found the button on the bottom shelf of a built-in bookcase that opened up a flight of stairs and caused a ceiling panel to slide open. I went half way up and peeked out into my new quilt studio. I stepped out onto the floor and the panel slid shut behind me.

I picked at the switch plate by the door that led from the house into the shop and sure enough, it was hinged like Larry said and lifted up. A push of a hidden switch opened the floor again and I went back down, pushed the button at the bottom and this exit closed. I went back to the first set of steps I had come down and flipped the switch there. Again as Larry had promised, the light came on and the panel at the top opened. I went up and popped back out into the living room. A press of the button that opened the bookcase caused it to slide back into position.

I looked around the sun-drenched room, feeling like I had just completed a trip to the outer limits of the universe.

CHAPTER 14

▼

The *Seinfeld* rerun was over. Henry was sitting on the TV facing me with an intent stare. It was a look I knew. "Okay, cat, we'll go to bed. Let me check the doors, then I'll be right there."

Cleo was curled on the foot of the sofa bed in her usual night-time snug little cat ball, sound asleep. I turned off the lights and went to bed. Even though I was tired, I lay awake for awhile thinking about how much what I had thought was my well-ordered life had changed in the last year. And here we are, I thought. Henry snuggled up next to me and I drifted off into my first night's sleep in my new house.

The next few days I spent rearranging the furniture and generally getting the kinks worked out. A trip to the Bedroom Specialist not only provided the bed of my dreams, I also got matching nightstands, a vanity and a dresser in exactly the finish I wanted. The bedroom furniture I had bought for the townhouse guest room went into one of the extra bedrooms. Inland Asphalt came and turned the rutted driveway into smooth pavement. I had the people from Apollo Spas come and check out the hot tub. It had been empty for several months and when I filled it there were a couple of leaks in the tubing for the jets. These were repaired and the heater was turned on. A hot tub was something I'd always wanted and the first soak was bliss. Henry and Cleo sat high on one of the carpeted platforms of the cat tree I had put in the kennel for them, Henry fascinated by the swirling steamy water, Cleo distressed; she just knew I was going to sink under the waves and drown!

Sunday morning I sat down with my checkbook. Henry and Cleo sat on the desk and helped—Cleo by trying to lie on top of my papers and Henry by knocking as many things off the desk as he could. His forward-pointing ears and whiskers told me how much he was enjoying watching things hit the floor. Occasionally he would jump down and pick up an object and carry it off with him or bat it around the floor like he was a hockey player, but most of the time he seemed content to just watch things fall. The third time my pen left the desk I shooed them outside.

"Well, I'm glad I still have about $8,000," I said to myself. "That's enough for a few months, but I need a job. It's time I took a look in the paper."

I went out into the living room and sat down and started reading through the classified ads. It was ironic. When I was an Licensed Practical Nurse, the big push was for Registered Nurses. I had started my nursing career as an LPN, but feared my position would be replaced by an RN. So I went back to school and got my RN degree. Now, there was more demand for the LPN than the RN. Like in Seattle, the hospitals in Spokane had become very money conscious. They were hiring more LPNs and unlicensed staff. There were few jobs for RNs listed. I decided I'd visit the area hospitals on Monday and at least get applications on file, that would be a start.

I glanced through the rest of the ads. The pets column was always one of my favorites. There were the usual kittens, puppies, birds, fish, and ferrets advertised. But, there was also a listing that caught my eye.

"Receptionist/assistant needed for vet clinic and crematorium. Must love animals, medical background a plus. Salary DOE. Resume to Bradley Mancusco, DVM, Box C-10, care this newspaper."

What the heck, I thought. That might be interesting. I went to the computer and wrote Dr. Mancusco a note.

CHAPTER 15

▼

Monday I went to town and filed job applications at the hospitals then did some shopping. It was so nice not to run into anyone who knew Phil. I hadn't seen him since that awful day in the townhouse. Once faced with the evidence, he had pled guilty to all the various charges against him, so I was spared the unpleasantness of having to testify in court. I read in the paper that he wouldn't even be eligible for a parole hearing for at least ten years. The last I had heard about him was that he had started his sentence at the state prison in Walla Walla.

Wednesday morning I was measuring windows for curtains when the phone rang. Dr. Mancusco wanted to know if I could come in for an interview.

"I own the All Animals Hospital and Crematory on Trent just east of Sullivan in the valley. Do you know where that is?"

"Yes, I do. I grew up in Spokane so I know my way around pretty well. That'll be easy for me to get to anyway, I live in the Mount Spokane foothills."

"Would this afternoon at three work for you?" he asked.

"That would be fine. I'll see you then."

Cleo was sitting in the middle of my bed grooming her whiskers. She greeted me with her usual meow. "So, Cleo, what do you think I should wear? This? This? You like the first one better? Okay, I'll wear it, but if I don't get the job it's your fault!"

While Henry only spoke when mad, hungry, or when needing my attention, every time I spoke to Cleo she spoke back. The pitch of the meows varied; I really felt like she was talking with me. It must have frustrated her when I couldn't understand her. Henry for the most part talked with his eyes. He was sitting by the front door and squinted his approval when I walked by him on my way out.

I had no trouble finding Dr. Mancusco's clinic, but I was surprised at the size of the building. It had an imposing façade with soaring columns and appeared to have a second floor with what looked like apartment windows above the entrance. Rather astonishing for an animal clinic. An even larger building stood behind the clinic. I wondered if that was the crematorium.

A bell chimed when I opened the front door and I heard a man's voice say, "Be right with you."

I took the time to look around. It was a typical vet's waiting room except for the lovely crown molding at the ceiling and the faux marble paint job on the walls. Two small offices opened off the waiting room, carpeted in deep pile in a rich blue. The marble floor was a bit of a surprise too. But, all the magazines were about animals and a rack of leashes hung by the front counter. The air carried a sharp medicinal smell with just a hint of the aroma of caged animals. A woman came out carrying a small dog.

"Thank you," she called over her shoulder, then smiled at me and left. A man came out of the exam room behind her.

Wow. A Viking. Tall, with broad shoulders, strawberry-blond hair and bright blue eyes that crinkled in the corners as he smiled at me. He held out a hand.

"Hi, are you Maggie Jackson? I'm Rick Evans. I'm Brad's partner. He's been delayed up at the cemetery, but he should be here soon. He told me to have you fill out an application then I'll tell you about the routine here. You can sit at the desk if you'd like. Give me a shout in the back when you're done."

He went back into the exam room. I realized I'd checked his left hand for a ring and been pleased not to see one. It was the first time in months a man had even looked good to me. Georgia had tried to fix me up with friends of hers a couple of times; the dates had been disasters. I didn't trust any man I met and didn't trust myself to make a good choice either. So I'd stopped trying. No more dates. It'd just be me and the cats. But now? Well, maybe.

The application was short, nothing like the ones I'd filled out Monday at the hospitals. I called out for Rick and he came back—he looked as good on second glance as he had on the first. He pulled another chair up to the desk and sat down.

"This is a regular veterinary clinic. We see all kinds of animals here and Brad and I both do farm visits. I see by your application you're an RN. Have you ever worked in a vet clinic before?"

"No, but I've always done a lot of doctoring of my own animals. Dr. Mancusco said something about this also being a crematory. Is that what that big building in the back is?"

"Yes. That's another facet of the business. A few years ago Hennessey Valley Funeral Home built this place for funerals and cremations. But, the deal fell through on the land next door that they had planned to use for parking. As you can see we can put about 20 cars in the front lot, but they knew they didn't have enough room for the parking needed for funerals. So, they bought some property on Pines and built a real nice funeral home and crematory and put this place up for sale. Brad bought it and remodeled the back of the building into the clinic. He also bought several acres of land about fifteen miles east of here that he's developed into an animal cemetery. That way we can offer cremations and urns to people whose pets die, as well as a place to store the ashes or bury their animals. We offer the same sort of thing that you would find at a cemetery or funeral home for people. At first the crematory seemed like it was much larger than we'd ever need, but we've had some people who wanted large animals, like horses, cremated and we were the only ones who could accommodate them. Washington state law prohibits the use of a crematory either before sunrise or after sunset, so Brad had to put in a special unit that causes the crematory to burn hotter than the usual 1000 to 2000 degrees in order to quickly do the bigger animals. Even so, it takes about four hours to cremate an average-size horse.

"The money he spent turned out to be a really good investment. The cemetery and crematory have some months generated more income than the clinic. Brad's wife, Lynda, pretty much runs that side of the business."

"I think that's a great idea," I said. "I've always buried my pets that have died, but it always bothered me that if I moved away they would probably get dug up eventually—I'd have much rather scattered their ashes. I bet lots of people like the cemetery idea too." I had to laugh. "I'm glad to know what this building started out as, I was a bit amazed by the outside and the décor in here."

"It is a bit of a surprise, isn't it?" Rick Evans was laughing too. "We don't even notice it anymore. Wait until you see the rest of the place. And yes, our clients do like the crematory and cemetery features. And of course cemetery clients tend to come back for regular vet care for their other animals, too. Come on, let's take a look around."

All Animals looked like other vet clinics I had seen, except for the marble floors and the continuation of the crown molding I had seen in the waiting room. This molding extended into small exam rooms with stainless steel tables and an equipment cupboard with a sink. Two rooms were set up as operating rooms, much like those in a people hospital, just smaller. The other side of the building had the kennel areas, dogs in a separate area from the cats. The cages ranged from quite small to several that would be large enough for a person to get in. Several of those also had outside doors that led to outdoor runs. Rick said they boarded a few animals occasionally, too.

After the tour we went back into the waiting room and sat down. Rick said, "Now, as far as the job you're applying for. What we need is someone to answer the phone, make appointments, write up the bills as people leave, accept payments, do phone triage, dispense medications, and handle some treatments on Mondays, Wednesdays, and Fridays. We keep Tuesday and Thursday without clinic appointments; those are the days we make farm calls and some house calls, but occasionally we might need you to work on either one or both of those days too.

"We also do a few outside appointments on the other days and there could be times when one or the other of us is out on a call and the one that's here might need some help with a procedure or in surgery. You would also probably get involved helping people choose urns and selling cemetery plots. Like I said, I'm Brad's partner right now, but his plan is to move to southern Oregon and start the same sort of business there. That's where he's from originally and he hates our winters here. I'm hoping to be able to buy his practice when he's ready to leave. Oh, here's Brad now," Rick said, looking up at the sound of the front door opening.

"Brad, this is Maggie Jackson," said Rick.

I stood up and held out my hand, "Hi, Dr. Mancusco, nice to meet you."

"Hello, Maggie. Please call me Brad—we're not big on ceremony here. Did Rick give you the grand tour?"

"He did, thank you. I think your crematory and cemetery features are great. I was telling Rick it's something I wished I'd known about last time I had a pet die."

"There're not too many facilities like this around. We even get animals' bodies shipped to us from all over the country that people want cremated and the ashes sent back to them in urns. Do you have any questions about what the job entails?"

"Rick mentioned bills and payments. That's the only part that scares me. I hope I wouldn't have to do any fancy bookkeeping. I've had no accounting training and I don't like it very much."

"No, you wouldn't have to do a lot of that. My wife is a bookkeeper and takes care of the majority of the accounting work. The bills are done on a template in the computer. All you'd have to do is fill in the blanks and give clients a print of their bill for that day's services, take in any payments, and give them a receipt."

"*That* I can do," I told him with a laugh. "The rest of the job sounds great. I've always been an animal person. And of course I'm familiar with most medical procedures—are they comparable to what we do with people?"

"Pretty much so. Why aren't you looking for a nursing job in a hospital?"

"I did put applications in at all of them, but there are not very many openings for RN's right now. Okay, now I have to climb on my soap box for a minute. The hospitals have gone to using so many unlicensed personnel that it's a little scary. Nursing assistants can be trained to do everything an RN does, but they don't know always *why* they're doing something and what the consequences of doing it might be. Each RN is then put in charge of a larger number of patients than in the days of primary care nursing and it's easy for a problem to get missed. The chance for a disaster is too high. Speech over," I said.

Brad smiled. Makes sense to me," he said. "Well, I'll tell you what, Maggie. I have a couple of more people to talk to. I'll give you a call probably by Friday afternoon and let you know either way, okay?"

"Sure, Brad, that'd be fine. I'll be looking forward to hearing from you. I'm curious though, is that an apartment on the second floor I could see from outside?"

"Yes, as a matter of fact it is, sort of. It's really just a bedroom and bathroom, but quite handy. When this was a funeral home they had somebody here at night to take any pickup calls. We use it occasionally when there's an animal that needs overnight monitoring. That has worked out really well."

"Yeah," said Rick. "The clinic where I did my post graduate residency work just had a lumpy sofa bed in the waiting room. This is like the Ritz."

I laughed and crossed my fingers on my way out the door. I really wanted this job. I could do quilting on Tuesdays and Thursdays and would even have time off on the weekends. The pay was not stupendous, but my expenses were few. This could really work out. I went home to await Brad's call.

CHAPTER 16

▼

Braaack, brack. *Braaack*, brack. The pheasant was at it again. I groaned and rolled over to look at the clock, not too bad, it was just six, but I knew he wouldn't let me sleep any longer. I got up and started coffee then went for the paper.

The Chinese pheasant who had decided my driveway was his turf was standing on the highest place he could find, a small pile of gravel left from the driveway paving job. He was surveying his domain and shouting his territorial ownership to any other pheasants who might dare to invade. His red head glowed like a beacon in the sunshine.

He eyed me cautiously when I opened the front door, then haughtily stepped away. He wasn't afraid, his arched neck and black-eyed stare told me, he just choose to leave his mound at that moment.

I walked out to the paper box, marveling at my little creek and listening to all the birds. Again, though, I had the sensation of watching eyes. Every time I had been outside since moving in I had the feeling something was there, observing my every move. The hair on the back of my neck prickled. There were cougars on the mountain, as well as bears and coyotes. The thought of a bear or coyote wasn't too frightening, a bear isn't especially sneaky, and I was too big for a coyote to seek out as a meal, but I would make a meal for a cougar.

I looked around, but saw nothing. I pulled the paper out of the box and hurried back to the house, trying to listen behind me the entire time.

The cats and I ate then I went to shower. I had just stepped out of the stall when I heard the phone ringing. I minced my way on soggy feet to the phone stand. One of these days I might learn to take the cordless into the bathroom with me.

"Hello?"

It was Brad Mancusco. "…so if that sounds all right with you I'd like you to start Monday morning," he finished. "We open for patients at ten, but the staff is usually here at nine."

"That's fine with me. I'm excited—this sounds like a great job."

"I hope it'll work out for everybody, Maggie. I'll see you Monday."

"Okay. I'll be there. Thank you."

I hadn't realized how worried I'd been about finding work until I found myself dancing around the kitchen, holding Henry and singing, "Mommy has a job, mommy has a job!" He complained bitterly about such treatment and Cleo came out to see what all the fuss was about.

"I'm going to work on Monday, Cleo. Isn't that great?"

"Meeee-yow, me-me-me YOW," was all *she* had to say.

CHAPTER 17

▼

Monday morning there was a film of frost on the windshield. It yielded quickly to the defroster, but I knew it wouldn't be long before snow flew. I was looking forward to it—I had missed the four cadences of seasons Spokane enjoyed. In Seattle soggy springs and summers with rare sunny days grayed into autumn, which then increasingly grayed into winter and I felt like I needed to check my skin for mildew. It was rare to have a blanket of white over slumbering flower beds and lawns and turning every tree into a Christmas card. I found myself anticipating the challenge of a true winter.

When I pulled into the clinic parking lot I noticed a plume of smoke coming out of a chimney at the back. The crematory must be running, I thought. I wonder how they get away with releasing smoke?

A woman looked up from the chair behind the reception desk as I came into the waiting room. She turned away from me and made a few quick taps on the computer keyboard, waited until a new screen came up then stood up and held out her hand.

"Good morning. You must be Maggie Jackson. I'm Lynda Mancusco. I'm sorry I wasn't here last week when you talked to Brad."

"Oh, that's all right. It's nice to meet you, too," I managed to stammer.

Brad was fairly tall, maybe just a little under six feet, slim, with a crisp, neat haircut. The day I met him he had been dressed with quiet elegance in an immaculate white lab coat over a tan silk shirt. Dark brown corduroy slacks hung neatly over polished ropers that I knew had never seen the inside of a stirrup or manure-caked barn floor.

Lynda, however, was a different story. She was short, and fat. Not stocky, plump, chunky, or full-figured, just plain fat. Rolls of flesh crowded her chin and her upper arms looked jelly filled. Her clothes, while obviously high-quality, were ill-fitting and soiled. A stained blouse gaped between the buttons and its tails dangled over stretch pants that screamed for mercy. Hair that had gone awhile since its last shampoo or cut hung in limp curls to her shoulders. Her eyes peered at me out of her cheeks like raisins pushed deep into dough. Rather than the glow of good health, her skin had a greasy sheen. A bulbous nose bobbed above lips that even while smiling looked petulant. Incongruously, a pendant that looked like a diamond-encircled ruby hung in the vee of her blouse, its delicate gold chain lost in the creases of her neck. What appeared to be full-carat diamond studs peeked out from her earlobes and her hands were lumpy with large-stoned rings. A diamond tennis bracelet sparkled on her wrist.

"I was just finishing up some accounts," she said. "Here, sit down. We have the appointment book in the computer. You can put it up in the corner of the screen so it's always readable. See? Then, all you have to do is fill in the blanks for printing a bill or a receipt. Got it?" Her fingers flew over the keys.

"You make it look so easy, but I'm not that computer literate. Do you have any kind of directions I can use to help me?"

Lynda smiled and turned the desk pad over. "Yes. I wrote some out for the last girl that worked here. She had never used a computer except to play solitaire and she did fine following these."

"That's super. I'm sure I can do it, too. Cheat sheets really help. Those are certainly beautiful rings."

She laughed and held out her hands. "Yeah, they look pretty impressive don't they? Well, except for my wedding set all my jewelry is costume. It would be too dangerous to wear the real thing." She held out her arm and pointed to the tennis bracelet. "It's *good* paste though. These are high quality cubic zirconia and the setting is electroplated gold. I paid a couple of hundred dollars for it. I wouldn't want to lose it, but not as much as I'd hate losing this many diamonds!" She laughed again.

She pulled the bracelet around on her wrist so I could get a better look at it. I noticed the clasp was the locking sort and there was also a safety chain. One of the stones caught a bit of light and flashed an instant of fire. I don't know, I thought, those sure *look* real. Oh, well, whatever. I just wish she'd wear the clothes to go with the jewelry. And maybe a shower and shampoo?

"I'm going to be here most of the morning and I'll help you with the first few clients to make sure you can do their bills by yourself before I leave," Lynda said. "You want some coffee?"

The phone rang. I nodded and picked up the receiver. My first day had started.

By lunch time I was feeling guilty about my harsh original assessment of Lynda Mancusco. Even though she could have used the help of a personal groomer, she did know her job. The computer sat up and barked every time she touched it, while I could hardly get its attention. Her interactions with clients seemed saccharin-sweet phony to me, especially when she was talking with people who had lost a pet and wanted it cremated and the ashes placed in an urn. But, I knew the approach worked when she showed me the very-healthy crematory and cemetery bank statements.

Wednesday Lynda left me on my own. She had a small office on the other side of the wall behind my chair containing another computer and several file cabinets. I could hear her tapping away at lightning speed. There was obviously a separate phone line there too, as I heard it ring several times. I hoped I could manage without having to bother her too much, and while I was slow I did all right. The first bill that dropped into the print tray was as pride-producing as a newborn.

For the first few weeks I spent all my time at the front desk. Rick and Brad seemed to be able to handle any crisis between them—at least until one day in mid-November. Brad called me at home and asked me to pick up some drugs from the veterinary supply house on my way to work. The supply house was west of town and after having to battle morning commuter traffic both ways, I didn't get to the clinic until nearly eleven.

The waiting room was full of people and animals. A tabby cat hissed out of her carrier at a goofy-looking young spaniel. Another dog hid shivering under a chair while a ferret oozed around in its owner's arms. Lynda was sitting in my chair talking on the phone. "Yes, Mrs. Cox, Dr. Evans is on his way to take those stitches out. It would help, though, if you could have your mare in a stall so he doesn't have to chase her all over the pasture again. Well, you do the best you can, then. Good-bye."

"Not to be funny," I said, "but this place is a zoo!"

Lynda looked at me blankly. "What? Oh, ha-ha. I get it. I'm glad you're here. Brad got called to a kennel where there's a purebred Newfoundland that's having trouble whelping. She's too big for the owner to try and bring in, so he went there. Rick is on the way to Horse Heaven Boarding Stables to take some stitches out of a horse's neck and I need you to take care of as many of these people as you can. There're some lab coats in the closet."

While I wasn't as tall as either Rick or Brad, I was tall enough that the lab coat didn't quite swallow me. I was ready to see patients.

The spaniel needed a new bandage on its back. Both its owner and I had to nearly climb on the exam table to get that happy, wriggling, dog to hold still for the few minutes in took me to replace the dressing. The dog had torn its back open scooting under a barbed wire fence. Brad had sewn it up as neatly as possible, but it had been a jagged tear. The places where pieces of skin were missing looked clean and healthy—the wound was healing well.

The hissing cat had been spayed ten days ago and all she needed were her stitches removed. Once away from the dogs, she became a purring, back-arching, face-rubbing sweetheart. Her owner only had to hold one hind leg up out of my way so I could get to the stitches. The cat lay happily on her side, purring and kneading the air with her front feet as I worked.

The shivering dog needed his claws clipped. With each crunch of the clippers he let out a hair-raising, pain-racked, howl. His owner laughed and told me not to worry.

"He always acts like he's being drawn and quartered in here," she said. "But I know what his howls of pain sound like, and these aren't it." While the noise was distracting, he did hold still. Once back on the floor he solemnly presented me with a paw to shake.

The ferret needed the tips of his teeth filed down. This would require a general anesthetic. Its owner left it for Brad to take care of.

"Assuming he gets back today, which I'm sure he will, he'll do those teeth and you can call us this afternoon and find out when you can pick up Slinky," I told the ferret owner while she helped me put him in a cage. On my way back to the waiting room I was thankful to hear Brad saying good-bye to a client.

"Well," he said, "My intention was to have you come back and spend a few days working with Rick and me before we left you alone, but it looks like you had a baptism by fire instead. How'd it go?"

"Really well, I think. Thank goodness there were no emergencies, though. I took out stitches, clipped claws, changed a dressing and admitted—if that's the word you use—a ferret for a tooth-filing job. Nobody bit me and the owners seemed satisfied."

"Sounds like you did fine," Brad said. "Go ahead and take your lunch break then you can help me with the ferret's teeth."

CHAPTER 18

▼

I had left my mother my new phone number and told her my schedule, but I wasn't surprised when the phone rang at six a.m. I was just glad it was a day off so I could go back to sleep if I wanted to.

It went just as I imagined. Once she ran down her list of objections to my divorcing Phil and "running home with your tail between your legs," she started in on my current life.

"...and you are a Registered Nurse. Why are you wasting your time in some foolish animal hospital? What sort of job is that?"

"It's one I like, mom. The hours are great, I can do some quilting, and I'm enjoying being away from the stress in the hospital."

"But what chance do you have of meeting a nice man ("doctor" I heard in her tone) keeping yourself locked away in a dog clinic?"

You haven't seen Rick, I thought. "Mom, right now I'm not interested in meeting any man. After what Phil did, it's hard to trust anybody."

"Well, I'm still disappointed. I hope you come to your senses soon. I have to go now—I have a lunch date and I need to go get ready."

I didn't argue with her about how much time she probably had to get ready for a lunch date, but just hung up the phone and noted my armpits were dripping. Talking to her was harder than digging ditches. I got up and crawled into the shower.

After standing under a flood of hot water until it started to run cold, I was ready to spend the rest of the day visiting the area quilt and fabric shops. I was surprised how many there were now and decided when I was ready I would just leave my long arm business card at the specialty quilt shops, not at all the fabric stores. I did not want to get too bogged down in quilting jobs, as I liked to be able to get the quilts back to their owners as soon as I could. Having someone else's masterpiece in my shop always made me nervous.

I visited Kaleidoscope Quilting and Home Décor, The Quilting Bee, Sew Easy Two, The Briar Patch, and Pacific Crescent Quilting. I knew about some other shops that were a ways away, like The Buggy Barn in the Reardon area and The Garden Gate in Cheney, but I decided not to go that far. As soon as I was ready I would leave my cards with the shops in town and in the valley. The owner of the Briar Patch had a longarm machine, so I wouldn't try to advertise there. First, though, I needed to decide on a name for my fledgling business and have some cards made.

It was a fun day, but it seemed the next morning came too soon. I was standing in the bathroom getting ready for work and in the mirror I saw the door behind me slowly opening without a whisper of sound. Henry had become quite skillful with doors and it no longer alarmed me to see one open as if by a ghostly hand. He walked into the room on his hind legs, his front paws up on the door, pushing. He hadn't yet learned to turn knobs, but I feared his figuring them out was just a matter of time.

He hopped on the counter by the sink and looked up at me. I knew this was my signal to brush him then pick him up so he could lick my nose or ear. A couple of dainty swipes was all he needed to give, but it was a necessary morning ritual for him.

"You want to go to work with me today, Henry? You seemed to like it there so much when you got your teeth cleaned that Brad said you can come as often as you like and be the clinic cat. What do you think?" This would be good for him. When I was home he would occasionally bring me some object he had chosen as that day's victim. It could be anything, from a crumpled piece of paper out of a waste basket to a wire coat hanger he dragged out for me one evening. On my days away he was obviously either bored or anxious; when I got home I would often find several odd items laid out on the floor in front of my chair. Henry needed a job.

Being a cat of few words, Henry purred and kneaded his paws. He made what he wanted obvious though, by racing ahead of me and jumping into the carrier as soon as I set it down.

"Okay, you can come with me." I looked around for Cleo. She was nowhere to be seen. I was sure she had gone into hiding the minute the carrier came out. Henry loved to travel; she loved the safety of home.

This being Henry's first visit to the clinic as the "house cat," there were lots of things he needed to do in the hour before patients started to arrive. He started by examining every corner of the waiting room. Then he pushed his way through to the exam rooms and kennel and cage areas. The dogs caused his tail to puff slightly, but he ignored the caged cats, and they him. His tour over, he jumped on the counter in the waiting room and curled his front paws under his chest— the most comfortable position from which to survey what he now saw as his domain. His neck arched in pleasure when Brad and Rick stopped by to say hello, but when Lynda approached to pet him he held himself rock-still. When she left I noticed that a narrow band of fur running down his spine was standing straight up.

CHAPTER 19

▼

I usually closed the skylight over my bed when I was ready to go to sleep so the room would stay dark until I wanted to get up. But, this morning when I opened it the light in the room scarcely changed. I went to the window and pulled the curtains aside and gasped with delight at the new white world I saw. It was my first snowfall since moving back. Henry and Cleo tiptoed around on unsure paws in their outdoor pen and were happy to come back in before I left for work. They had no idea what this strange white stuff all over the ground was. Henry was intrigued, but Cleo almost knocked him down getting back into the house when she realized that not only was this stuff cold, it became wet, too.

I gave myself extra time, but found the roads not as slick as I had feared. When I pulled up in front of the clinic there was a huge cloud of smoke hanging over the building. When I walked in Brad and Lynda were standing in the waiting room.

"Don't the environmental people get after you about all that smoke? I never saw that much before."

"Morning, Maggie," said Brad. "No we don't have any problems because that's not smoke. It's just steam. We have all sorts of scrubbers in place to prevent any particles from getting into the air. You're only noticing the steam so much because it's cold out. During warm weather you can hardly see it. Sort of like the paper mill on Argonne. Go by there some cold morning; it looks like the place is burning down."

"Oh, good. That makes me feel better." I glanced at three large boxes in the corner.

Lynda saw where I was looking and stepped in front of them. "These are dogs that have been shipped to us for cremation. I'll be putting their ashes in urns and shipping them back to the clients. You needn't concern yourself with them."

I didn't think I had looked particularly concerned, but I let it go. Lynda was extremely protective of what she considered her animal crematory/cemetery business and Brad was busy enough with his clinic practice that he usually let her do what she wanted. There could be no argument with the fact that she was an astute businesswoman—the crematory/cemetery part of the clinic was very profitable. Besides, the thought of dead animals in boxes gave me the creeps anyway. I was happy to let Lynda take care of them.

My job had become easier and the computer and I became friends. There would probably never be a time that I could put it through its paces like Lynda did, but it no longer took me five minutes to print out a bill or receipt. This gave me more time to work in the back. It was great to see an animal wake up from anesthesia, start to eat and drink again, and get ready to go home. I especially liked handing these pets back to their grateful owners. The times an animal had to be euthanized were sad, but helping their owners know that they had made the best decision for their pet's sakes was gratifying in its own way.

Christmas had come and gone, now it was late January; where had the time gone? I had been spared an ordeal with my mother; she had gone to Ireland to spend the holidays with Beth. I was in trouble about that, though, she just could not understand that I had neither the time nor the money to take off for two weeks like she wanted. I would have loved to have seen Beth and the kids and hoped to be able to get to do that in the future.

It seemed like the leaves had just started to fall and now we were all looking forward to spring. The winter had been beautiful, lots of snow-decorated scenery, but we were ready for a break. Cold, wet, weather is hard on animals and on the vets that have to attend to them. Now I knew why Brad had installed a gas burning pot-bellied stove in his office. Whenever he or Rick had to make a farm call that was the first place they headed when they got back. The flames would be turned up all the way and they would sit in front of it toasting their frozen feet and drinking coffee or hot chocolate.

I saw Brad's truck go by the clinic and heard him come in the back door to his office. A minute or so later the intercom on my desk clicked. "Maggie? Would you please go in the back and get my shoes? I changed into my boots back there and forgot to bring them out. Do you mind?"

"No, Brad, not a bit. Let me finish this bill and I'll go get them."

There was a sort of mud room that opened to the outside of the building for all the outdoor gear. Brad and Rick would shed their muddy boots and wet coats there when they got back to the clinic. The room had been part of the original crematory where the caskets were brought in and I had to go through the door that connected the crematory area to the clinic to get there. I knew Lynda was working, so I was surprised when the connecting door did not open when I turned the knob. I knocked and called out.

"Lynda? It's Maggie. Are you there? Brad needs his shoes."

"Yeah, hang on a minute."

The lock clicked and the door opened.

"Thanks, Lynda. I just need to…"

"No," she put up her hand to stop me. "What do you want back here?"

"Brad's shoes. He said he left them in the mud room and asked me to get them for him."

"Okay, you wait. I'll go get them."

She shut the door in my face and I was surprised to hear the lock snap into place again.

"Here." Lynda opened the door just far enough to hand out Brad's shoes. "I'll get his boots later." She shut and locked the door again.

I took Brad his shoes. "Does Lynda always lock herself in the back? She wouldn't even let me in far enough to get these."

"Thanks, Maggie. Yes, for some reason she likes to do that. Maybe she's afraid a client will accidentally wander back there, I don't know. But she's the one who does the bulk of the work, so I don't argue with her. Besides, she's not the type you want to have mad at you. I learned that years ago—the hard way." He chuckled. "We were just starting to market the animal crematory and cemetery services. I had objected to doing mail order and web site business advertising for animals to be sent to us for cremation—I told her I was afraid people would think it was tacky. She became enraged and didn't speak to me for days. Then when she did start to talk, she said she'd chop me up in pieces and dispose of me in the crematory. She was going to be successful and *nobody* was going to stand it her way."

A shiver went up my back. I could imagine Lynda doing just that. I managed a weak smile, "That does create some mental pictures. I don't care if she locks the door—I was just curious why."

"Well, it makes her happy. When she's happy we make money and it's hard to argue with that."

He put on his shoes and went to see an ailing cat. I went back to my desk.

CHAPTER 20

▼

There was a burial at the cemetery and Lynda was not at the clinic when the UPS man came. He had four large boxes, which I knew contained the bodies of animals to be cremated. Boxes that big, probably dogs, I thought. I held the door for him and looked at the boxes as he carried them in. I noticed they were all from a town called Nowlan, in California. Without really knowing why, I wrote "Nowlan, CA-4" on a piece of paper and put it in a plain file folder in the back of a drawer.

The next few days were busy and I forgot all about the dogs from California until Lynda reminded me.

"You know those four boxes that came in the other day?" she asked. "I'm finished with them. I called UPS for a pickup, but they probably won't be here until late this afternoon. I have to go talk to some people about a plot for their horse, so I'll be gone. When he gets here tell him the boxes are by the back door, as usual."

"Sure, Lynda. See you later." I watched her drive away. Henry had just eaten and needed to go and find a place to dig in the dirt. I slipped him into his harness and took him out. He would wait until I had my back turned before choosing a desirable toilet spot so I obligingly faced the building. The boxes were sitting on the porch by the back door.

Letting out more leash for Henry, I wandered over and looked at them, curious about who in California had four large dogs that all died at the same time. But, the boxes were not addressed there. Instead they were going to addresses in Anchorage, Alaska; Pueblo, Colorado; Sandpoint, Idaho and Shelby, Montana. Now I really *was* puzzled. I wondered if I dared ask Lynda about this. But after thinking about it for a few minutes, I decided not to. She could be so touchy about this part of the business that she thought of as hers. When I went back in I added the destinations of the boxes to my earlier note in the file folder I had stuck in the back of the drawer.

By the time Lynda came back I had forgotten about the boxes of dog ashes. A woman and her eight year-old daughter brought in their kitten that had been hit by a car. It took all of Brad and Rick's skills to put the tiny animal back together and I was kept busy with the other clinic patients. By five o'clock I was more than ready to lock the doors and head for home. The kitten was sleeping off her anesthesia in a cage. Brad was confident that she would be fine with a few days of healing time. The child and her mother had left—shedding tears of relief. Henry knew it was time to go too, he was sitting by his carrier trying to pick the door open.

"Okay, kitty, give me a minute and we'll be ready to leave." I turned off the computer and sat and watched the screen fade to black. As tired as I was, I found myself wishing that the evening held more than dinner with the cats and a book.

"Not much info there, Maggie."

I jumped. "Rick! You scared me. No, I guess there's not. It suddenly seemed like too much of an effort to even get up to go home. What a day."

"Yeah, it's been a wild one, hasn't it? I'm not much in the mood to go home and have a TV dinner myself. Say, there's a new restaurant on Argonne, the Thai Grill. I heard the food's great. Want to try it out tonight?"

"Meow!" The usually silent Henry said. I looked over at him and he was bobbing his head up and down.

"Well, Henry wants to go anyway," said Rick, laughing.

"And I'd like to too, but," I looked down at my crumpled pants and blood-streaked blouse. "I think I'd need to go home first and change."

"Me too. I sweat like a butcher while Brad and I worked on that kitten. Tell you what—you go on home and change and so will I. Then I could pick you up around seven? I have an apartment just up Forker Road from the Progress Road intersection so I'm not that far from your place. Give me some directions."

I grabbed a notepad and sketched out a map and handed it to him. "Does that make sense?"

"Sure, I know where this is. I'll see you in a bit."

"Okay, Rick. It'll be nice to get out a little. Henry, you'll have to stay home, though."

"Meow," he said and nodded at me again. I could have sworn he was smiling.

CHAPTER 21

▼

I stopped on my little bridge and got out to get the mail. Once again I felt eyes on me. This time when I turned to look I didn't see anything, but did hear a rustling in the bushes.

"Go away, cat," I yelled, stamping my feet on the planks. All was silent. Feeling foolish, I turned to get back in the car.

"Scared ya, huh?"

I gasped and jumped so hard I almost inhaled my tongue. Who in the world was this?

"I never been called a cat before." A tiny woman stepped out of the brush. Her eyes snapped black and her mouth was open in a silent laugh. She walked up to me and stuck out her hand. "Betcha thought I was a cougar, huh? Sully's the name, now don't be calling me Sally, hear?"

"Okay," I managed to stammer, "Nice to meet you."

"Didn't want to scare you, but I didn't want to say hello until I knew you was okay. I been watching you since you moved in. Eleanor was a friend of mine and I was worried what sort of trash might buy her house, but you seem okay. Got any whiskey?"

"Uh, no, not right now, but I'm not very well supplied yet. Do you live nearby?"

"No, I walked here from Rathdrum—what do you think?"

"That was dumb question, sorry," I said, "but you certainly surprised me."

Sully cackled. "That I did, that I did. Well, I'll be getting on home; I live just up the hill a ways. Soons as you have a minute, come up for a snort, or maybe some tea?" She crooked her little finger in imitation of a duchess holding a tea cup. "But I'll be putting coffee in that. I'm across the road, first place uphill from here."

Before I could reply she melted back into the bushes. Feeling a bit dazed, I went in and changed my clothes for dinner with Rick.

"I met a neighbor, Henry. It will be interesting to see what you think of her." He just squinted at me then curled up to take a nap.

CHAPTER 22

▼

Rick gave me a snip-by-snip account of the kitten's surgery on the way to The Thai Grill. The last stitch went into the skin as he pulled into a parking place.

"We were lucky—most of the injuries were awful to look at, but relatively minor. She didn't have any broken bones and no major organ damage. It just took lots of sorting out and suturing to put her back together. She'll be a funny looking little thing until her fur grows back out, but then she should be fine. Let's go in and get something to eat—I'm starved."

The Thai Grill really was new, as was obvious by the minimum décor. Plain covered tables sat in an over-lit room and huge bare windows that begged for curtains looked out on the parking lot. But the aromas coming from the kitchen made the rather stark room unimportant. I sighed with contentment with the first spicy bite of Thai curried chicken.

"This is heaven," I told Rick. "I'm glad you suggested this. I'm so happy the kitten's surgery went well too. The little girl who came in with it was so upset."

Rick nodded. "It'd be nice if all our cases turned out that way, that's for sure. So, how do you like animal medicine now that you've had a taste of it?"

"So far I love it. Even the animals we can't save I feel good about. You know, if a human being gets hit by a truck or becomes old and miserable there isn't anything that we can do to lessen their suffering much. I've seen so many people die by slow agonizing inches and have heard people begging to have the pain stopped. Sometimes I think we are nicer to our animals than we are to our people."

Rick took a sip of his drink and carefully set the glass down. He stared at it for a minute, then said, "That's mainly why I decided to become an animal doctor rather than a people doctor. I watched my father die of bone cancer and saw how his doctor suffered almost as much as my father. As my dad's pain got worse his doc gave him as much pain medication as he possibly could without actually killing him. I think the drugs made dad's death came sooner, for which I'm very grateful, but he still suffered longer than he should have had to. I remember how his eyes looked when he would beg us to put him out of his misery. Now when I see that same look in an animal's eyes it's like I'm finally helping my father when I can relieve the animal's suffering with one quick injection." Rick picked up his drink and took a long swallow. "Whew! Sorry to dump that on you all at once." He looked up and I saw tears in his eyes.

"Oh, that's okay." I said, "I've had similar experiences myself and I know how awful it can be. I remember the first time I know I hastened a patient's death. This woman had been horribly injured in a car accident. She wasn't fully conscious, but she still was writhing in pain. She looked like she was screaming, but there was no sound because she had an endotracheal tube in and she was on a ventilator. Her doctor was amazed she had even lived long enough to make it to the hospital. Her family begged us to do something, anything, that would help. Her doctor explained to them that her injuries were so severe that she could not survive. He told them that if he prescribed enough pain killers and sedatives to make her comfortable that it could actually cause her to die quicker. They didn't want her to die, of course, but because they knew she was going to regardless, they told him to give her as much medication as she needed. He wrote the orders for morphine and Valium. Some families like to stay with the patient and some don't. This woman's family chose to stay.

"I signed out the drugs I needed then started giving them. With the third series she finally started to become calmer. The fourth doses gave her enough relief that she was able to come to for a few minutes. She seemed to understand her family when they told her they loved her and said good-bye. She was still in obvious pain, though, so they asked me to give her more drugs. I warned them what might happen and they understood. Those last doses allowed her to slip away, pain free, I hope.

"When I think about it I can still feel the hug of gratitude her mother gave me. That was a good death. Too many after that weren't." I took a shaky breath. "Boy! I guess it's a spill-your-guts-night for me too."

We finished our drinks and ate our dinners in silence, lost in our memories.

I watched the waiter clear away our dishes. "I think it's definitely a dessert night. Do you suppose they have ice cream?"

While we spooned chocolate-laced vanilla, I asked Rick about Lynda and the crematory business.

"So, she advertises all over the country and people send their animals to be cremated, is that right?"

"Yes. They choose an urn from a catalog or off the website, and put the order with the body of their pet. She puts the animal's ashes in the urn, seals it shut and sends it back to them."

"That's what I thought. But, the other day UPS brought four big boxes that all had the same return address on them, Nowlan, California. I'd never heard it, so I looked it up in an atlas. It's a small town in the southern part of the state, with a population of less than 10,000. That seemed a bit odd, but then today those urns went out, but not back to Nowlan. They went to four different states. Why would someone in California send animal ashes all over the country?"

"I don't know. It's too late for Christmas."

I couldn't help laughing. "Oh, Rick, that's awful! Seriously though, what do you think?"

Rick shrugged. "That's a part of the business I've never paid a lot of attention to. Brad seems to be content letting Lynda handle it—she *has* made money for him."

"That's another thing. Not that I've really searched, but as near as I can tell there is nothing in the computer about her part of the business. No bills, no statements, no customer lists, no accounts payable, no accounts receivable, nothing except for was on the bank statements she showed me. I hope she's not trying to pull a fast one with the IRS. I'd hate to see Brad get nailed for tax evasion."

Rick frowned. "Lynda's always been kind of secretive. She probably has records that she keeps on disks rather than storing them in the hard drive. But, I'd never thought about her trying any kind of a tax dodge. If Brad gets in trouble, I would too. We *are* partners, after all."

"I was going to try to ask Lynda a few questions today, but by the time things calmed down enough that I could have, she'd left. Maybe I can talk to her tomorrow," I said.

Rick shook his head. "I wouldn't if I were you. The last front desk person we had got too curious and Lynda made her life so miserable that she finally quit. It'd probably be best to keep track of things that seem off to you, then if you find out that she is skimming money or something, I'd talk to Brad about it. Although I don't know if he'd confront her or not."

"She really has a lot of power over you guys, doesn't she? I never realized it before. I already started a file in fact, about those four boxes I saw. I'll let you know what I find out."

Back home I sat in bed with the Spokesman-Review. Below the fold on the front page was a story about a group of local teenagers who had gotten hold of a particularly strong batch of cocaine. One kid had died of heart failure and several others, while expected to recover, were in the hospital. The policeman who had been interviewed for the story was saying how easy it was for anybody to get illegal drugs.

"Marijuana to heroin, doesn't matter," he said. "They want it, they can get it." I shook my head. What a waste of a young life. It didn't seem to matter how hard the law tried—as soon as one source of drugs was eliminated another popped up to take its place.

CHAPTER 23

▼

"Excuse me?"

Startled, I glanced up and saw a man in a long coat with a cap pulled almost down to his eyes standing at the counter. I had been so focused on the computer screen that I hadn't heard him come in.

"Yes? May I help you?"

He peered around the room. Well, I hope so. Is Dr. Mancusco or Mrs. Mancusco in? Can I talk to either of them?"

"I'm sorry, but neither one of them is here right now. Could I give them a message or is there maybe something I could help you with?"

He looked confused and distressed. When he reached into his coat pocket I found my finger inching toward the panic button that was wired to the clinic's security company. As the frayed wallet came into sight I relaxed. He opened it and pulled out a card.

Handing me the card, he said, "Cecil Willik, my niece is Sandra Cochran." He looked at me, waiting.

I wrote down the name on his card. He was still watching me.

"Is she one of our clients?" I asked him.

"No, she used to work here. Don't you know her?"

"I've only been here a few months. Was she the receptionist?"

He nodded. "I used to get a letter or a call from her nearly every week. She and I are all that's left of our family. But, I haven't heard from her in a long time and when I tried to call her I found out that her phone had been cut off. I'm worried about her."

This must have been the woman Rick told me about, I thought. "Let me see what I can find out. Would you like to sit down?"

"No, I'll just wait here," he pulled off his cap and started to twist it in his hands.

The personnel files were in Brad's office. Sandra's contained all the relevant paperwork. There was a short typed note signed by Lynda. It was dated July 16 and said, "Sandra Cochran did not show up for work this morning. There was a note on her desk July 15 stating that she was resigning, effective immediately. A check for the pay for the hours worked to that date will be mailed at the end of the current pay period." Another note said that the check had been sent and cashed. There was a photocopy of the check in the file. I did not find Sandra's resignation letter. I took the notes and went back to my desk.

"These were in her file, Mr. Willik. It looks like she quit rather abruptly. There's no mention of any other contact with her after July 16."

Cecil Willik walked unsteadily to a chair and sat down. "None of this makes any sense. Sandra would never just walk away like that. She was particular about always giving at least two weeks notice whenever she left a job. I went to her house, too. There was a notice on the front door saying that the bank had fore-closed on the mortgage. I don't understand that, either. She saved for years to buy that house; she'd never stop making the payments. I've been all over trying to find out where Sandra is. My motel room number is on the back of the card. Please have either Dr. or Mrs. Mancusco call me as soon as they can." He groaned to his feet and plodding steps took him out the door.

I watched him drive away in an old pickup.

"Who was that?" asked Rick, coming up behind me.

"Rick, I was just going to intercom you. That man said he's Sandra Cochran's uncle. It's been awhile since he heard from her, so he came to see her. But, he isn't having any luck finding her."

"Sandra, yeah. She was the receptionist we had before you. She's the one I told you about who got too curious about the crematory business and Lynda managed to get her to quit."

"These were in her file," I said, holding up the papers I'd found. "It looks like she just took off. What has her uncle concerned, though, is that she hasn't kept in touch with him. I guess she's all the family he has left and he's worried about her."

"I remember Lynda talking about getting some calls from Sandra's bank about her house. She walked away from that too, Lynda said. Lynda bragged about get-ting rid of her. She said that Sandra's walking out on her mortgage proved what

Lynda had said about her all along. I hadn't gotten to know Sandra very well—she was here such a short time—but she seemed nice enough." Rick shrugged. "She'll turn up eventually. Probably ran off and got married and is having such a good time that she forgot all about her poor old uncle."

"But she quit making her house payments, too, Rick. That sounds a little funny to me."

He shrugged again. "You never know about some people."

The next morning I gave Cecil's message to Brad. He called him from the phone on my desk.

"I don't know anything about where Sandra went, Mr. Willik," Brad said. "She never called or came in after that last day, but she did cash her final paycheck. I'm sorry, Mr. Willik, that's all I know."

CHAPTER 24

▼

It was the middle of February. I woke up with a strange feeling of heaviness and sadness. I got up and stumbled to the kitchen. Coffee will help, I thought.

It didn't though. What was the matter with me? I sat and stared out into the snow-choked back yard. Dry, dead flowers rattled in the wind and empty tree branches scratched at the cold gray sky. It wouldn't be long before the spring rains came and washed away the snow, I hoped. I was ready for a change.

I got up and refilled my cup, trying to figure out where this sadness was coming from. I had a new house, a job I liked, and I was starting to think about making quilts again. I should be feeling great. Idly my eyes went to the calendar. I counted on my fingers. My baby would have been due about now, that was what was wrong. I crept back to bed and let the pillows soak up my tears.

By noon I felt better. I had cried myself back to sleep and awoke to find the sun shining through the skylight. I went back to the kitchen and stuck a cup of leftover coffee in the microwave. Now the view out the window looked different to me. Those dry flowers I would cut down when spring came and there were buds visible on the tree branches that would soon be green leaves. A chickadee hoped across a mound of sparkling snow, picking up the bits of seed the bigger birds had dropped while eating at the bird feeder. It didn't look nearly as desolate outside as it had earlier.

At work we all had enjoyed the snowy winter, but we were just as glad to have it nearly over. Warm weather would be nice, but we knew it would be late May before the last streaks of white high in the hills finally gave way.

February was its usual bleak and wet self, but it drizzled away into March, then April, and all of a sudden spring was here. The soft, mild days brought a deluge of work for Brad and Rick. Animals large and small were giving birth and many times needed help. Cows were calving, sheep were lambing, dogs were whelping, cats were kittening. New life was everywhere.

Spokane and the surrounding communities had large horse populations and nearly every day there was a mare in trouble or a new foal to examine. I was still keeping track of as many of Lynda's deliveries and shipments as I could. I had collected a lot of information, but hadn't had the time to really sit down and look at it.

By the end of June the flood of baby animals had slowed to a trickle. Brad looked exhausted and I was glad when he told me to not schedule anything for the week of July fourth. He and Lynda were going to take some time off and visit friends on the west coast. Lynda had the June month-end statements ready to go; she told me to mail them on the first of July. Brad gave me the week off with pay and I was ready for a break. Because I needed to be on call while they were gone, I couldn't go anyplace myself, but that was fine. The time at home would be great. I had scarcely been near my sewing or quilting machines during the busy months at the clinic and I could feel a quilt twitching in my fingertips.

All I had to do was check the answering machine twice a day, call Rick for emergencies, and help him if he needed it. There were some animals still recovering from injuries or illnesses and a few boarders. Rick and I took turns going in to check on them and make sure they had food, water, and clean cages.

July first was my day. I made rounds of all our patients and boarders and was picking up the box of statements to go to the post office when the phone rang. I stood and waited until the answering machine clicked on.

"Brad, this is Helen Barnes. I need you to call me back as soon as you can. Shep's torn his side open on a nail that was sticking out of a fence post. I got the bleeding to stop, but I know he needs stitches. Please let me know when I can bring him in."

I picked up the phone before she could hang up. "Hi, Mrs. Barnes, this is Maggie. Brad is out of town, but Rick is on call. I'll let him know you have an emergency and he'll come in. I'll call you right back."

Within an hour Shep was lying quietly on the exam table. The cut in his side was not deep, but it was long and jagged. Rick gave the big dog a sedative and started stitching. I was kept busy trimming away the fur on either side of the wound and holding the edges of the skin together while he worked.

We snipped and sewed for over an hour and finally Rick was done. Not exactly the kind of sewing I was craving, but it was good to see Shep's skin go back together. I went to run Mrs. Barnes' bill while Rick put a dressing over the wound and told her how to take care of her dog.

I pushed the power switch on the computer and waited for the barking dog sound that would tell me that Windows98 was done loading. While I waited, I went to get Mrs. Barnes the antibiotic ointment and the written instructions she would be needing. I slid everything into an envelope for her and went back to my desk.

Instead of the usual desktop wallpaper of a laughing Labrador, I saw a message telling me there was an incorrect disk or drive and that Windows98 had not been properly shut down. I looked at the tower and could see a floppy disk in drive A. I popped it out and Windows98 finished loading. Curious, I put the disk back in. There were only three files on the disk. I picked one and I opened it. A list of names and money amounts appeared on the screen. This was information I had never seen before. None of the names were familiar and the dollar amounts after each one were no less than $1,000. What *was* this? And where did it come from? I ejected the disk again and looked at it. The label was blank except for the letters LM-4. Was this Lynda's file of crematory records? I could hear Rick and Mrs. Barnes' voices, they were on their way out. Quickly I grabbed a blank disk and went to "copy disk." Two clicks and a buzz later I had a duplicate of Lynda's disk. I dropped it into my growing file of crematory information and found the correct program for Mrs. Barnes' bill. By the time they came out with Shep it was ready for her. She wrote a check and Rick helped her make her dog comfortable in the back seat of her car.

"You be sure and call if you have any problems," he told her. "We're checking the answering machine at least twice a day while the clinic is closed."

She waved her thanks and drove away.

Rick came back in, looked at me and said, "What?"

"Am I that obvious? Well, I think I found some of that data we had talked about that night at the Thai Grill. Lynda must have accidentally left a disk in this computer. I remember she was having some trouble with her monitor and did some work out here just before they left. Do you want to take a look at it?"

"Yeah, I do. Like I said, I could be in as much trouble as Brad if she's pulling a fast one with the taxes. Let's see what you found."

Once again the list of names and amounts were on the screen. Rick didn't recognize any of the names either. The second file on the disk had a list of names and addresses from all over the country and the third had what appeared to be a list of expenses. I printed out the address list and got out my hand-written list of pickups and deliveries to the crematory. It didn't take long for us to see that all the deliveries to us came from southwestern states, California, Arizona, New Mexico and Texas. But, none of the packages that had been sent out had gone back to where they originally came from, they went all over the country. Rick and I looked at each other.

"Does this make any sense to you?"

He shook his head. "No, not a bit. But I'm one of the bookkeeping impaired. How does this compare to the clinic's records?"

"I'm a bit impaired too, but I can see that these records don't look anything like the regular ones. I don't see any records of services provided or bills sent and there are so many identical amounts. I don't know, though. Maybe she only operates on the cash-at-time-of-service principle. That would explain the absence of statements. At least she's keeping records of income and expenses, although I don't see any sign of quarterly taxes being paid. But what I'm really curious about though, is why somebody in Virginia would want the ashes of a dog that died in California."

"Let's see that list of places the dogs come from again. I wonder…hang on a second, I think I have a road atlas in the car." Rick went out and came back in with a large book and opened it out on my desk. "I was right," he said. "Look. All the states the dog bodies are coming from share a border with Mexico."

"Okay, I see. So what does that mean?"

"She couldn't be that stupid," he muttered.

"I'm lost. Stupid? What do you mean?"

He turned and looked at me. "Think about it. What's something that people are constantly trying to get out of Mexico and into the US?"

I felt my jaw drop. "Drugs? Are you thinking she's involved in smuggling *drugs?*"

He nodded. "It would be a perfect setup. The stuff gets sent here in the dead dog boxes, she packs it in urns and ships it off. Did you notice how the names of the people she receives payments from keep repeating? Hard to imagine the same people having that many dogs die."

"But how would they get the drugs across the border? Aren't the guards at the crossing points pretty vigilant about checking?"

"Yeah, they are. I don't know how the stuff could get into the country. That would be the hard part. I'd sure like to get a look in one of those boxes. Hey, Brad left me his extra set of keys in case I needed to get into his office. He keeps extra supplies of controlled medications in a cabinet in his office. He does that so if the place gets broken into the thieves wouldn't get everything. Let's see if we can open up the back."

Before I could even react Rick was on his feet. By the time I got to the door to the crematory area he had the door to the rooms open and was inside.

Lynda had a stainless steel table in the outer room that looked like the same kind of table I had seen in the hospital morgue that was used for human autopsies. It had channels down both edges of the table that led to a drain that went into the floor. Against one wall was a cabinet of instruments and a pair of sinks. The opposite wall was stacked with boxes of urns, each labeled with its size and description. A large cooler like I had seen in hospital morgues took up another wall. Everything in the room was very clean. I could hear Rick in the next room. I went to see what he was finding.

I had never seen a crematory before. It didn't look elaborate. A large square door was centered in an unpainted cement block wall. To the right of the door a shallow shelf built from the same blocks jutted out. Above it was a temperature gauge, a timer, and buttons labeled START PROCESS and STOP PROCESS. On the floor on the other side of the door various size racks leaned against the wall. Rick opened the door and looked inside. He motioned for me to come look too.

"You can see where the door's been enlarged and the inside altered to accommodate large animals. Those racks over there slide along those rails that go all the way to the back. The cremated remains fall through into the tray in the bottom, then Lynda can empty the tray into the urn the person has chosen. It looks like the rack she has in there now is for something the size of a big dog. Nothing interesting here that I can see. There's a trace of ash in the bottom, so we know she does do cremations. She keeps this area a lot cleaner than I would have given her credit for, though."

He shut the door. "She had me help her one day. This is pretty simple to operate. After you slide the animal in on the tray all you have to do is close the door. It's really heavy, but the way it's counter-weighted it shuts and latches by itself with little effort. Then you push the start button, the door locks, and the process starts."

"Let's get out of here, Rick. Even though I know she and Brad are in Seattle this gives me the creeps. I expect her to walk in on us any second."

"Yeah, me too."

We went back to the front desk. I picked up the computer printouts and began to look at them again.

"You know something, Rick? Lynda's going to be suspicious when she gets back and realizes she left that disk out. I'm going to need to find a secure place to keep this file I've put together. If she is involved in something like drug smuggling and finds this stuff, brrr, gives me the shivers. I bet our lives wouldn't be worth a nickel to her."

"You're right. Let's make another copy of everything. I'll put it in my safety deposit box at the bank. I'll write out our suspicions and put everything in an envelope. I'll write on the front that the envelope is to be opened in the event of my death. My mother is the executor of my estate and has the other key to the box. That way if we end up dead at least the police will know where to start looking."

"That sounds a bit dramatic," I said.

"Yeah, but we need to be prepared. You wouldn't want her to get away with killing us, would you?"

"Of course not."

"Well, if she found evidence here she'd destroy it and us too."

"You're probably right. The safe deposit box sounds okay, but what are we going to do in the meantime? Should we call the cops?"

Rick sat and thought for a minute. Then he shook his head, "No, not yet. We don't really have any proof for them and if they come snooping around that could be disastrous. Let's see if we can get them some. Maybe we can manage to get a look inside one of those boxes that are delivered here, or one that's going out, for that matter."

"That would be a good place to start, for sure." I sighed. "I had hoped this would be a nice, peaceful, job. Now I feel like quitting and going back to a people hospital. At least there I wouldn't have to think about getting arrested, or maybe even killed."

"Please don't quit, Maggie." Rick stood up and pulled me to my feet. He wrapped his arms around me and hugged me tightly to his chest. "I'd miss you too much. I'm going to need your help to figure all this out. Besides, if Lynda ends up in jail we'll need someone here to do her job. I know that some of the crematory/cemetery business is legit and that Brad would like to continue to offer those services."

With my heart hammering so hard I was afraid he'd feel it, I stepped out of Rick's embrace. "Oh, I'm just babbling, Rick. I'm not going to quit—at least not right away."

I picked up Lynda's disk and wiped it off. For all I knew she'd check it for finger prints when she realized where she had left it. I put it on the desk by the computer, willing my hands to stop shaking.

"But, we can't be too careful either. Now, if I'm going to be Nora to your Nick I expect perks. Dinner tonight?"

Rick laughed and nodded. "You're on!"

CHAPTER 25

▼

I knew I didn't want to take any of this stuff home with me and after considering and rejecting several ideas, I decided to hide the file I was compiling in the dropped ceiling over the waiting room. I was just tall enough to lift a tile and set the file on top of an adjacent one. Hopefully that would be a place Lynda wouldn't think to look should she get suspicious and decide to search the clinic.

The rest of the week was uneventful from a clinic standpoint. I had hoped that a dead dog box would come and maybe Rick and I could get a look inside, but no such luck. The only delivery that came was a new monitor for Lynda's computer.

I wondered, too, if Rick and I were being just a bit dramatic assigning Lynda a role as a drug smuggler and potential murderer. The more I thought about our tour of the crematory area and the conversation about drugs and murder the crazier I decided I was.

Rick and I spent part of every day together during Brad and Lynda's time away, either at the clinic or out and around. He was still fairly new to the Spokane area and we spent enjoyable days touring. I took him past the house on the South Hill where I'd grown up and showed him the schools I'd attended. It was fun to drive up the road on Moran Prairie that was named after my great-great-grandparents on my father's side who had cut it through and homesteaded there. Rick had been to Riverfront Park many times, but had never seen any of the 'before' pictures of the site, so we spent one afternoon at the library looking at the pictorial history of the park's development. There was a western art show in the convention center that occupied us for another day. We discovered we had much the same backgrounds and enjoyed many of the same things. Rick started dropping hints about wanting to further the relationship, but I was skittish. After my experience with Phil it would be awhile before I would dare to trust another man with my heart.

Lynda and Brad came back to work looking rested. I wondered what she would say when she discovered that she had left her disk in the front office computer. I didn't have long to wait.

She took her new monitor into her office and I could hear her opening the box and the clicks and snaps as she set it up and turned it on. There were a few moments of silence then I heard her open and close her desk drawers. Next she rummaged through the closet. I heard her walk across her office and go through her desk again. Then she burst out of her office and went to my computer, her eyes riveted on the disk I had left lying next to it. I was standing at the file cabinet and watched her out of the corner of my eye. She glanced from side to side then picked the disk up. She started to put it in her pocket, then stopped.

"How'd this get out here?"

"What, Lynda?" I turned away from the file cabinet praying that my face wouldn't give me away.

She held up the disk. "This was on the desk by the computer. Have you been looking at it?"

"No, I'd never seen it before. It was in the drive when I went to boot up last week and I had to take it out. I needed to run a statement for Helen Barnes and that info's all on the hard drive. I saw your initials on the label so I figured it was yours."

She took a step toward me and I had to fight the urge to back away from her. "You'd better be telling me the truth, Maggie."

I drew myself to my full height and looked down on her; she looked less threatening that way. "Lynda, I resent the implication. What's on that disk, anyway? State secrets?"

She laughed, but the frost in her eyes did not thaw. "No, just Brad's and my tax records, that's all. I'm the private sort and don't like to think about people snooping in my stuff."

"Well, Lynda, I'm not a snoop. Besides, you're the one who must have left that disk in the drive anyway. Remember? You came out here and used this computer after your monitor went down."

Whew, I thought. My bravado seemed to have worked. Lynda's expression looked less forbidding and she nodded slightly. "Yes, you're right. I guess I must have left this out here. Sorry if I overreacted, Maggie." Without waiting for an answer she went back into her office.

Suddenly weak-kneed I sat down. It was easy for me to imagine Lynda mixed up in criminal activity—she had a palpable ruthless quality about her. Maybe I wasn't so crazy after all.

CHAPTER 26

▼

The next morning I decided to walk up the road and visit Sully.

I saw "Sully Hendrickson" on the mailbox outside the first driveway on the other side of the road from me. She had a bridge too, but hers just spanned a rocky drainage ditch. Her house was an old A-frame, tucked into a mass of trees. I couldn't really tell if there was anybody home, but halfway up the driveway a huge ball of fur that I hoped was a dog flew off the porch and ran toward me.

"Buffy! It's okay," I heard somebody yell, and then Sully stepped out her front door. "Come on up, he's all hair and no tooth," she said. Buffy had stopped by the porch and just sat and looked at me. At least I assumed he was, I couldn't really tell which end was which.

"I just put the coffee on, how do you take it?" Sully motioned me in. Her living room looked like a man's delight of a hunting lodge. Dusty trophy heads covered the walls and there was what I assumed to be a bear skin on the floor in front of the fireplace.

"Yup, me and the old man had some good times in here," Sully cackled at me. "That there bear hide got a bit of use."

Too much information, I thought, as I followed her into the kitchen that was a cheery yellow, with a large round table in the middle. She handed me a thick white mug of coffee and offered a roll.

"Just baked 'em this morning," she said. "So, how're you liking Eleanor's place?"

"It's perfect; I love it."

"I seen those big boxes being moved into the shop, what're they about?"

For the next hour Sully and I traded information. I soon realized she was the news hound for the area. She was able to tell me who lived where, what they did for a living, and how she felt about their moral character. It was an interesting morning. I was finally able to get away, feeling drained of everything I ever knew. But, I could see where Sully could be a valuable asset. I knew I liked her too, when I saw the cats that lounged about her house and the obvious Buffy bed on her sofa.

"You all come back any time, now," she said as I left. "I git kinda lonely here at times. Wore out two husbands, but don't really want another one."

"If there's anything I can help you with…" I started to say, but she interrupted me. "No, I do okay here. Got my little pickup to run around in and as longs as I have food and my Johnny Walker for an evening toot I'm good."

Home looked a bit dull after the morning with Sully, I had to admit.

CHAPTER 27

▼

Three days later UPS delivered two boxes to the clinic, both from one address in Arizona.

"Sorry about that one box," the driver said. "It tipped over in the truck and one corner got crunched. Be sure and let the office know if there's any damage."

"Thanks, I will." I said as I signed for the boxes. The corner of one *was* crunched and split. This could be Rick's and my best chance to get a look inside. I looked around. The waiting room was empty. Brad and Lynda had left for lunch. There might not be another opportunity like this.

I went to the back and got a flashlight. Rick was almost done neutering a cat and I told him about the damaged box.

"Give me a couple of minutes, Maggie. I'll get this guy into a cage then I'll come help you."

While I waited for Rick, I moved the boxes so that we would be able to see the front driveway. If Lynda and Brad came back while we were busy we'd need the few seconds of warning.

"I think if we drop this box on that corner again it might split some more and then maybe we can see inside," I told Rick.

"That might work. Here, let me try it."

Rick lifted the box. "Boy, it's fairly heavy. Okay, here goes." He picked the box up and dropped it onto its damaged corner. The cardboard corner was pushed in further and one of the pieces of tape holding the top flap in place broke.

"Hey, I think that did it. Let's see if we can tell what's inside."

Rick put the box back on top of the other one. He lifted the edge of the flap up and I shined the flashlight in. "What can you see?" he asked.

"Not a lot. It looks like a black plastic bag. Let me see if I can get my hand in…"

"Wait," he said, "Let me tip the box so what's inside will shift toward the corner."

"That worked. I still can't see much but I think I can reach in and feel…YUCK!"

"What is it, Maggie?"

"I don't know," I said, rubbing my fingers up and down my pant leg. "It felt sort of hard and soft at the same time, and very cold. Maybe it really *is* a dead dog."

"Uh-oh, Brad and Lynda just pulled in. Quick, take the flashlight and go sit at the desk—pick up the phone or something. I'll be in back cleaning up after that neuter job, okay?"

We shoved the boxes away from the window and Rick disappeared. I grabbed the phone and punched in the numbers to my bank's automated teller service and got my checkbook out and flipped it open. By the time Lynda and Brad came through the door I was pushing buttons and writing things down. I heard Lynda say, "What the heck…"

I hung up the phone. "Oh hi, did you guys have a good lunch? Lynda, those boxes came while you were gone. The UPS man said he dropped that box in the truck and it popped open a little bit. The phone's been busy, so I didn't get a chance to look at it. He said to let the office know if there's any damage to the contents. I didn't tell him what was probably inside."

Lynda stood unmoving for a minute. Then she picked up the box and headed toward the back. "Well, there's really no way to damage a dog's body by dropping it. And as long as the owners don't know what happened it won't matter. I'll be out in a minute for the other one."

I picked up some files and turned to put them away with the distinct feeling of having dodged another bullet.

That night after dinner Henry was helping me in his unique cat way to clean up the kitchen. I grabbed him just as he started to eat a rubber band.

"Give me that, you little stinker. Don't you remember what happened last time you ate one of those? I thought we were going to have to cut you open…" Wait a minute. I dropped the slimy rubber band in the trash and kissed the complaining Henry on the head. "You just gave me an idea, you slippery devil, thanks!"

I set Henry down, but before I could get back to loading the dishwasher the phone rang. It was Rick.

"We never got a chance to talk this afternoon," he said. "We still don't know anything do we? If that was a dead dog for Lynda to cremate where were the drugs? I'd be willing to bet the box would have been searched at the border."

"I've been thinking about it too, and I have an idea, thanks to Henry. Maybe the drugs came across the border inside the dogs."

"I'd thought about that too, but even so I'd think they'd find it."

"Wait, Rick, I wasn't finished. I meant what if the drugs came over inside the dogs *before they were dead?* Remember a couple of years ago those guys who were trying to smuggle cocaine by putting it in balloons then swallowing them?"

"Yeah, that's right. Didn't one of the guys die or something?"

"Uh-huh. One of the balloons burst inside him. But what I was thinking is that maybe somebody feeds drug-filled balloons to dogs. Then they'd bring the dogs across the border, kill them and send them to Lynda. She'd retrieve the drugs and send it off in the urns. Then she'd cremate the dog and throw the ashes away."

"That's a gruesome idea, Maggie. Although I must admit, a good one. But it's a pain to bring a dog in from Mexico, all kinds of paperwork are necessary."

"I know. That's the part I can't really figure out. I thought maybe the smugglers were taking dogs *into* Mexico then bringing them back full of drugs. But, they'd have to have a bunch of dogs and a reason to be making frequent trips in and out of the country with one. I don't know—I'm stumped."

"Now what we need to do is intercept a box and take a good look at what's inside."

"This is scary stuff, Rick. Is it time to talk to the police?"

"Yeah, maybe. My neighbor, Tom, is a deputy sheriff. Let me run all this by him kind of unofficially and see what he says we should do. I'll see you in the morning. Sleep well."

"Like after this conversation I have a chance of that. Okay, Rick, you sleep well too."

I lay for over an hour watching the leaves blowing in the wind, their motion turning the moonlight that shone through my skylight into strobe flashes, before I felt sleepy enough to close it and try to go to sleep.

CHAPTER 28

▼

The man in the neat blue suit had "cop" written all over him, so I wasn't surprised when he said, "Hello, I'm Detective Stan Watson, Sheriff's Department. I need to speak with Dr. Mancusco." My stomach did a flip/flop. Had Lynda been found out? Was this seemingly innocent vet clinic the center of a drug smuggling cartel?

Brad came out and took Detective Watson into his office. After a few minutes the intercom on my desk chirped. "Could you come here for a minute, Maggie?"

The detective sat by Brad's desk with a notebook open on his knee.

"Remember the day that…" Brad started.

"Let me ask the questions, please, doctor. Maggie Jackson, is that right?"

"Yes." I said around the lump in my throat. "Is something wrong?"

"I don't know yet," said the detective. "I understand you had a conversation with a Cecil Willik a couple of weeks ago. Could you repeat it for me?"

I sagged with relief. This wasn't Rick's neighbor investigating drugs like I'd feared.

"Well, he said he was Sandra Cochran's uncle and that he hadn't heard from her in awhile, which he said was unusual. He told me she had been the receptionist here, so I pulled her file. I told him there'd been no contact with her after July 16th, her last day here. He left his card and asked me to pass the message to the Mancuscos. Then he left." I finished.

"And you haven't talked to him since?"

"No. Nothing's happened to him, has it? He looked so tired and worn down when he was here."

The detective shook his head. "No, he's okay, but worried about his niece. He filed a missing persons report and I'm doing the preliminary inquiry." He stood up and closed his notebook. "You have my card, Dr. Mancusco. Be sure and call us if you think of anything else. Thank you too, Ms. Jackson."

He shook hands with both of us and left. I turned to Brad. "It was all right for me to talk to Mr. Willik and show him those notes from Sandra's file, wasn't it?"

"Oh, sure, that was fine. I gave the detective copies of everything, too. It was odd the way she quit. She'd been so dependable and responsible until then. Lynda didn't like her though. She thought she was nosy." Brad sighed. "Lynda can be a hell-cat at times. If she decides she doesn't like someone, well…anyway, she made life around here so miserable for Sandra that she left. I just assumed that she'd found another job. I can't imagine where she'd be."

"People do funny things sometimes, Brad. Are the police going to let us know if they find her?"

"Yes. I asked Detective Watson to do that. Now I'm curious, too."

CHAPTER 29

▼

Once again leaves were showing yellow through the skylight at home and Henry and Cleo were growing their winter coats. It didn't seem possible that we would be looking at six months of cold weather again so soon. Short-haired Henry didn't look much different, my fingers just sank deeper in his fur. Cleo, however, looked like she had stuck her toe into an electric outlet. Every long hair on her body stuck straight out. With just her paws visible she rolled around the house like an animated fur ball. As the nights grew cooler they were less interested in staying out in their cat yard and more intent on my bed. I never needed to open the heat register in the bedroom—two cat bodies pressed against me kept me plenty warm.

I went outside and picked the last of the apples off the gnarled old trees. It didn't seem possible that I had been in this new place and new life for almost a year.

Over those months Rick became an ever-more-important presence. Seeing him deal with all kind of situations at the clinic had given me a unique window into his personality. I had seen tears in his eyes after putting a badly injured dog to sleep and wondered if he was remembering his father. The children who accompanied their pets into the clinic adored him. No matter how busy he was, Rick always took the time to tell the kids what was going on with their animals.

One winter day he shivered his way home after a stray cat had kittens in his coat before we could get her into a cage and another time he took a litter of orphaned puppies home every night for a month to bottle feed them.

Rick also seemed to know without my having to tell him that I wasn't ready to get romantically involved with him. We dated like friends—dinners, movies, picnics in the park. He helped me landscape my yard and wallpaper the kitchen. Wallpapering can kill a relationship quicker that cheating, but we got through the project without a single argument.

I got lots of hugs and kisses but no pressure to go further. This made me care for Rick more than endless vows of eternal love would have.

After three years with Phil I hadn't known as much about him as I learned about Rick in one. I was starting to trust again.

The pace at the clinic was steady. Lynda continued to get boxes nearly every week from one or another of the southwestern states. My file in the ceiling was getting thick with speculation. Rick's neighbor said we would need some hard evidence before the police could get involved.

Then an opportunity presented itself. UPS came early and Lynda wasn't in yet. I knew this would be a chance to get hold of a box. But, she came in the door just as I picked it up and started toward the back. My plan was to put it in one of the kennels that had a curtain over the front then come back and get it after the clinic was closed. I had gotten as far as the door to the kennel area when she stopped me.

"Where do you think you're going with that?"

"Lynda! You startled me. I was just taking this…"

"Obviously," she said. "Put that back where it was."

"I was trying to help, Lynda. It doesn't seem like a good idea to leave these sitting out too long. I didn't know when you'd be in and I was going to put them by the back door. A couple of weeks ago a client's child almost had one open. That wouldn't do much for customer relations, now would it?"

While she could be nasty and abrasive, I had figured out that Lynda did not do well with confrontation. She was a back-pedaling coward, and proved that again.

"Yes, I suppose you're right. Okay, from now on you may take my deliveries and put them back by my door if I'm not here. But don't be poking around in them. I always open the boxes under a hood wearing gloves and a mask to help prevent contamination."

"You don't need to tell me that. I'm certainly not interested in coming in contact with a dead animal if I can avoid it."

"Good. I'll get these boxes out of here," she said.

I watched her load them on a hand truck and go into the back. I heaved a sigh of relief. That had been close. I wondered if Rick or I would ever have a chance to investigate one of those boxes.

He and I talked every day, either at work or in the evening. I was in bed watching TV when he called that night. I told him how Lynda had almost caught me making off with one of her boxes.

"But, actually it may have been a good thing," I told him. "She's now willing to let me move them back to the crematory door. Maybe she's trusting me more and I'll have more opportunities to learn something."

"Possibly. You need to be careful of her though. If she thinks you're curious she'll set you up and you'll get fired—or hurt. I don't trust her at all."

"I'll be careful, Rick, don't worry."

"Well, I do. I care a lot about you, Maggie. I don't want anything to happen to you before you have a chance to get to like me better."

"Oh, Rick, I *do* like you."

"Yeah, but not enough. Well, it's getting late, I'll see you in the morning. Good night."

Henry jumped up on the bed and coiled himself next to my shoulder. I nestled down under the covers and thought about Rick. The more time he and I spent together the more I found myself liking him. Maybe it *was* time for me to take a risk. I sighed and drifted off to sleep.

"Help me!"

I awoke with a jolt. The night around me was dark and silent. But I was sure I had heard a voice. I lay still, listening. Dainty clicking noises told me Cleo was having a drink of water from her dish in the bathroom. Henry grumbled in his sleep and wiggled himself into a more comfortable position. I heard a car go by on the road. No calls for help. But as I listened, I remembered the dream.

I was in a strange house with a bunch of teenagers. Somehow I knew I was in the living room of a house in Sandpoint, Idaho. It was night and there was a party going on. I didn't know if my role was as a chaperone or if I was merely an unnoticed observer—dreams are always so disjointed. But I did notice that the kids kept going into a back room for brief periods. One of the boys came out and staggered up to me. He looked like he had dipped the lower half of his face in flour, it was coated with a white powder. "Help me," he said.

Abruptly I saw myself standing on the shore of nearby Lake Pend Oreille. Looking out into the dark, I could see the face of the boy who had asked me for help floating above the black water. I could hear his cries fading away into the night.

I was sweating and shivering at the same time. It was the voice in the dream that had awakened me. But why was I dreaming about drug-using teenagers? There was nobody I could think of that I knew from Sandpoint and I'd never had any exposure to the drug world. Drug world? The image of Lynda Mancusco carrying a box out of the waiting room clinic came to me. I rolled over and grabbed the phone.

"Rick? It's Maggie. Hey, I'm sorry for waking you up in the middle of the night like this, but I just had a weird dream. Did you see the story in the paper awhile ago about the kids that got hold of the extra-powerful cocaine at a party up in Sandpoint? One of them died and several others were really sick. Well, I just dreamt that I was in Sandpoint at a party when one of the kids came up to me and asked for help. His face was covered with white powder—I think it was supposed to be cocaine. Then, I got an image of Lynda with one of her dead dog boxes. Rick, one of those first boxes going out of the office that I noticed the addresses on went to Sandpoint. If she is a drug middle-man she might be responsible for that kid's death. We have to stop her if she is!"

"Whoa, Maggie. Give me a sec. Yeah, I do remember hearing something like that. And I thought we *are* trying to figure out what Lynda's doing and stop her if we can, aren't we?"

"Yes, I guess I now have a real urgency to want to stop her. That dream's going to bug me."

His yawn was audible. "Yes, I can see where it would. Let's continue doing what we're doing and see what we can learn. We need to be careful though. Don't let your anxiety make you careless. If she's doing this she's probably making a bundle and will do anything to keep the money flowing. Let's both get some more sleep. I'll see you in the morning."

"Okay, Rick, thanks."

I hung up the phone and tried to go back to sleep. But my whirling brain kept me awake. The sky was beginning to lighten and the morning birds were starting to sing before I was able to doze off.

CHAPTER 30

▼

Friday morning at last. I was glad the week was ending. Trying to find out what Lynda was doing without tipping her off as well as tend to all my clinic duties had worn me out. Brad and Rick were having me help out in the back more often, which made it hard to get the front office work done. Lynda had also been very busy both with her mysterious boxes and what I had started to think of as "legal" cremations and animal funerals. This morning her office phone seemed to ring constantly. It was a relief when it was time for her to put her answering machine on and go to lunch.

She came out of her office carrying her purse. "Maggie, I'm expecting an important call, but I have an appointment at the cemetery. I'm going to leave my phone on and my office door open. Please answer it and take messages. If a Clyde Owens calls please tell him that I can meet him and his wife at the cemetery tomorrow at two as planned."

"You have to work tomorrow? That doesn't sound like any fun."

"It won't be too bad. It's the only time this guy and his wife could both come out to choose a plot." She smirked, "He won't know he's paying extra for my time."

I watched Lynda drive away. There went my lunch-period respite. Maybe this was a chance, though. I could copy any other floppy disks she had.

The cemetery was about twenty minutes away. Even if she went there and came straight back I'd have at least forty minutes. I switched my phone to the answering machine and went into her office with a handful of blank disks. My hands became sweat-slick as I opened her disk box and put the first one into her computer. Each one only took ninety seconds to copy, but it was ninety seconds of eternity. As I completed each copy I took it back out to my hiding place in the ceiling. The last one was copying when her phone rang.

"All Animals Hospital, may I help you?"

"Hello? This is Clyde Owens. I'm trying to reach Lynda Mancusco. Is she there?"

"Hello, Mr. Owens. No, Lynda had to step out. But she asked me to tell you if you called that she can meet with your and your wife tomorrow at two like you'd planned."

"My wife…? Oh, yes, yes, good. Tell her that'll be fine, thanks."

I hung up the phone and took the last of the disks out of the computer. My time was almost up. I put Lynda's disk away and was reaching for the copy when I heard the front door open. "Hi, Henry. Where's your mommy?" Lynda was already back.

I froze. I had no pockets, there was no place to hide the disk. Lynda was almost at the door. A stack of files on the corner of her desk inspired me. I shoved them off onto the floor.

"Maggie! What do you think you're doing in here?"

"Oh, Lynda, I'm so sorry I made this mess. I just got off the phone with Clyde Owens. I gave him your message and when I started back out I knocked these over. I'll pick them up."

"No, never mind, I'll do it. Clyde didn't have any questions did he?"

I leaned over the files scattered on the floor and with a flick of my wrist slid the disk under Lynda's desk. I bundled up some of the files and set them back on her desk. "No, he said tomorrow's fine. Are you sure I can't help…"

"No!" she interrupted sharply. "You go on back to your desk." She slammed the door behind me.

She finds that disk and I'm dead, I thought. Then I had another thought. Is that what Rick was talking about? Was she actually setting me up so she would have a reason to get rid of me? Not that I couldn't find another job, but I liked this one. Plus, if she was smuggling drugs I *had* to help stop her.

It was one of the slowest afternoons of my life. Lynda was in her office the entire time. I kept waiting for her to come out with the guilty disk in her hand, but by the time the clock finally snailed its way to five o'clock nothing had happened.

"So what do you think? You feel like going out to eat tonight?"

"What? I'm sorry, Rick. Did you say something?"

"Maggie, where are you? I've been standing here talking to you for five minutes. I asked you if you want to take Henry home then I'll pick you up for dinner."

"I'm a bit distracted, sorry. Sure, let's have dinner. But let's leave Henry here and go in your car, okay?"

"Sure, I guess. But how come? I didn't think you liked leaving him here."

"I'll tell you later, shhh, here comes Lynda."

"It's after five, Maggie. Are you about done?"

"Yes, Lynda, I am. I'm beat. I can't wait to get home and into some comfy clothes. I hope you don't have to spent too much time with the Owenses tomorrow." I saw Rick open his mouth and frowned at him. He closed his mouth and walked into an exam room.

Lynda watched me while I turned off and covered the computer, switched the phone to the answering machine and picked up my lunch bag and purse. Henry was sitting hunched up under my desk. He looked at me solemnly and opened his mouth in a silent meow. Praying that he would stay there quietly, I put my coat on and left. Lynda stood in the doorway, watching me walk across the parking lot. I watched her in my rearview mirror; I could see her head turn as she tracked my car, I knew her eyes followed me until I turned onto Trent.

About a quarter of a mile from the clinic there was an old access road. I backed in and waited. All I could do now was hope that Rick would leave the clinic and head for his apartment. After ten antsy minutes I gasped with relief when Rick drove by. I pulled out behind him and tooted my horn. The first chance I had I pulled out and passed him, flashing my lights as I went by.

A ways down Trent from the clinic was an Excell Grocery Store. I made sure Lynda's blue Suburban was not behind me then I flicked on my turn indicator and pulled into the parking lot. I found a spot and went into the store. Rick joined me in front of the meat case.

"What the hell's going on, Maggie? I thought we were going take my car and go to dinner."

I looked from side to side, it was like Lynda had tracked me here and was listening to everything I said.

"I know, but this afternoon Lynda had me answer her phone while she was gone. I took the opportunity to copy her disks. She came back sooner than I expected and nearly caught me. I had to leave one of the copies behind—it's under her desk. There was a stack of files on the corner of the desk—I knocked them off to distract her while I hid it. She's either afraid I saw something in those files or she's getting suspicious, I don't know. Anyway, I didn't want her to know we were going to be together. She watched me like a hawk until I left. Let's go grab a quick bite to eat then we'll go back to the clinic. I have to pick up Henry so I have an excuse to be there. Do you still have Brad's extra keys?"

"Yes. I planned to give them back to him today, but we got busy and I forgot. This makes me nervous, Maggie."

"It makes you nervous? Geez, Rick, I'm scared to death! Let's get out of here. I'm not really hungry, but I want to give Brad and Lynda plenty of time to leave before we go back to the clinic."

Rick and I went to Shari's. The food there was always good, but I may as well have been eating sawdust. We finished eating about six thirty. "They must be gone by now," I told Rick. "Give me the key to Lynda's office."

He handed me a ring with six keys on it. "It's one of those, but I'm not sure which. You'll have to try them all. But you should have plenty of time. I'll follow you and make sure you get in and out okay."

"Thanks, Rick. Although if you hadn't suggested it I was going to ask you to."

We stopped at Excell where I had left my car. Rick followed me back to the clinic. The parking lot was empty. With knees almost audibly knocking, I opened the front door and disarmed the security system. Henry was sitting on floor next to his carrier, waiting for me.

"Just a minute, fella. I need to get something then we'll go home." I went to Lynda's office and tried the first key. No luck. The second one wasn't it either. By now my hands were damp and shaking so hard it was all I could do to fumble the third key into the keyhole. It was the wrong one too.

"Yow, YOW." Henry howled from the waiting room. Startled, I dropped the keys on the floor. Shit! Now I was going to have to start over. I grabbed the key ring off the floor and pushed the first key I had a grip on into the lock and turned it. The door clicked open. Weak with relief, I went into Lynda's office.

I dropped to my knees and started to feel around under her desk. My hand closed over the disk. I pulled it out and stood up. Now to get out of here and lock the door again.

"What are you doing here, Rick?"

Oh, my God. Lynda was here. But where? I couldn't see her, but it sounded like she was standing right next to me.

"Maggie just stopped by to get Henry, Lynda. She should be right out."

I looked around, frantic. Oh. Her office window was open a crack. That's why she sounded so close.

"But what are you doing here, too?"

"Maggie and I had decided to have dinner tonight. She left Henry here and just came back to get him."

"I'll just go in and see if she needs any help." Lynda said. I heard the front door open. Must hurry, MUST HURRY. My feet were encased in cement. It was all I could do to walk out of her office and lock the door behind me. Henry was in his carrier. I shoved the disk under the pad he was sitting on and stuffed the bunch of keys into my pocket. The fur on his spine was standing straight up and his tail was a black bottle brush. Lynda came through the door just as I latched the carrier door.

"Lynda? What are you doing here?"

She glared at me. "That's just the question I have for you," she said.

"Rick and I went to dinner and I didn't want to take Henry with me. I just came back to get him," I told her, hoping the tremors in my gut wouldn't make my voice shake.

"The alarm went off." Lynda was walking around the front office looking at everything. She tried the door of her office—it did not open.

"But I know I disarmed it. It must not be working right."

"No, it's working fine." She looked at me unsmilingly. "I changed the code."

"Oh, I didn't know that."

"I've been worried that someone's getting in here when we're closed. I'm not telling anyone the new code. If you ever need to come in after hours you'll have to call me to meet you here."

Henry was picking at the pad in his carrier. I tapped on the top to distract him then picked him up. "Okay. If I'd known I'd have called you tonight. Come on, Henry, let's go home."

Lynda walked up and looked at Henry. He flattened his ears and hissed at her. "Snotty beast, isn't he?"

"No," I said, "I think he got spooked being locked in here by himself. Sorry to have caused you any trouble, Lynda. I'll see you Monday morning."

Rick was standing in the parking lot. "My house," I whispered and walked by him to my car.

Once home I shut my front door and sagged against it in relief. I went in the bedroom and peeled off my sweat-soaked clothes and struggled my way into a swim suit. If there was ever a time I needed the hot tub it was now.

"Yow-ow!"

"Henry! I'm sorry, kitty! Here, you can come out." Tail held aloft, Henry stepped out of his carrier. He went to the mud room jumped with fluid grace to the counter where his food waited. Cleo appeared out of nowhere and joined him. While they munched I took a tray to the refrigerator and got a bottle of wine. Glasses joined it and I took everything out to the deck. Rick pulled into the driveway and parked his car in the spot behind the house next to where my vegetable garden had been.

He nodded when I waved the wine bottle and went into the house to change into the swimming trunks he kept there. Within minutes we were soaking and sipping.

"I was trying one of the keys when Henry yowled. He probably thought he was warning me that Lynda was coming. Instead of a warning though, he startled me. I dropped the keys and had to start over. Then, I thought I was going to wet my pants when I heard her voice at the front door. It sure was a good thing you were able to stall her for the few seconds I needed to get out of her office. God, I hope I never have to go through anything like that again."

"You and me both," Rick said. "She gave me the third degree for about ten minutes after you left. I think she finally believed me when I told her we'd had dinner and to make sure that you didn't have any trouble I followed you back here to get Henry. She had to agree with me that the clinic's not the safest place to be at night. But, did you get the disk?"

I nodded. "I pushed it into Henry's carrier about a half a heartbeat before she came in the door. You should have seen him, though. All prickled up! He never has liked her—he's probably always known what she is doing."

The hot water and the wine worked its magic. By the time we'd finished the wine and watched a movie on TV I was feeling normal. It took all of my resolve not to ask Rick to stay—it would have been so nice to be able to cuddle up with him. But, in the end I cuddled with Henry, and slept well.

CHAPTER 31

▼

Saturday morning the air had a distinct nip. Fall was definitely here and winter wouldn't be far behind. I had suffered through the previous winter with a Seattle winter-weight coat and at times thought I was going to freeze to death. Today before it got any colder would be a good time to look for a new one.

The Factory Outlet Mall in Post Falls, Idaho, had just been an idea when I moved to Seattle. But, in the years I'd been away it had become a big, bustling place. There were at least three outer wear companies represented. I was sure I'd be able to find something I liked at a price I liked, too.

A short distance from the mall was the Greyhound Park. I had never been to a dog race and didn't care if I ever went to one. But from the looks of the parking lot, not everybody felt that way. I hoped conditions had improved. There had been distressing news stories in The Seattle Times about dogs that no longer won races being killed and their bodies thrown in dumpsters. The dogs that were found dead appeared to have been in good health and there was quite an uproar about them being destroyed. The stories spurred the creation of an adoption service. Whenever possible dogs that had outlived their racing years were placed with people who wanted them as pets. We had a few of these dogs as patients. They were beautiful—bone-thin, with soft elegant coats and intelligent eyes under luxurious lashes. For the most part they were calm, gentle animals, spending much of their time each day sleeping. Maybe I could get one now that I had a fenced yard, I thought. It would be nice to have an early warning system at my rather secluded house.

The Outlet Mall was a rabbit hutch of stores, placed cheek by jowl regardless of type. A kitchen supply store snuggled up against a store that sold nothing but socks. A clothing store was next, then another kitchen outlet. There was something here for almost every need, from fancy to ordinary. As I had hoped, I found the perfect coat. After all my walking from store to store I was hungry. I stopped and had a sandwich. While I ate I thought more about a dog. I didn't get out this way very often and the race track was so close. I decided to drive over and see if they had any information about the Greyhound adoption program.

The parking lot was huge and almost full. I found a spot in the back and started walking toward the main entrance. About halfway there I saw a blue Chevrolet Suburban. I stopped. If this was Lynda's, I was going to turn around and go back. The experiences from the night before were still too fresh in my mind.

I crept up on the car, feeling like I was sneaking along like Henry did when he discovered a killer electric cord on the floor. I sidled up to the Suburban and peeked inside. There was a child safety seat in the back and the remains of a McDonald's Happy Meal on the front seat—this wasn't Lynda's car. I stood up straight and chided myself for being stupid. She had never mentioned going to the dog races, and with the number of people around even if she happened to be here I stood little chance of running into her. Besides, I remembered with a glance at my watch, she had an appointment at the cemetery this afternoon. I walked on toward the building.

In the lobby I found a stack of pamphlets about Greyhound adoption. I dropped one in my purse and decided that since I was here I might as well look around a little.

It was between races and the track was empty. It felt to me like a shrunken, indoor horse racing venue. People were milling about sipping drinks and discussing favorites and odds. I was able to see a few of the dogs—they looked as healthy as the ones I had seen at the clinic. The next race wasn't due to start for an hour. I decided not to stay for it and turned to go back the way I'd come.

My car keys had a talent for migrating into the deepest recesses of my purse and I stopped in the lobby to dig for them. A steady stream of people were coming through for the next race, so I stepped over against the back wall to get out of the way. I finally pulled my keys out and was heading for the front door when a familiar voice stopped me in my tracks.

"So, you think you'll have another matched dozen ready to go out pretty soon?"

A chill went up my back. That was Lynda's voice. My God, she was here after all. Carefully I looked around. She was nowhere in sight. There was a closed door to my left marked 'private'—that must be where she was. A man's voice answered her, but I couldn't make out any words. Terrified of being discovered, I turned and walked out of the building as fast as I could without attracting attention. I forced myself to walk rather than run to my car. Then I had to watch the speedometer all the way home—my inclination was to floor-board the accelerator. My driveway had never looked better.

I spent the rest of the day cleaning and doing laundry. Henry and Cleo napped outside in the sunshine. They wouldn't mind a dog, I was pretty sure. Phil and I had done some dog sitting for friends a couple of times and both cats had put up with him fairly well. Plus, their outdoor run was completely enclosed, so when they were outside they couldn't be chased. I was glad for the extra tall chain link fence around the entire back yard. Greyhounds like a large exercise space, but it needed to be a secure area. Clients had told me that a runaway Greyhound was nearly unstoppable.

I had found some lovely blue fabric and a soft yellow floral print in my stash of fabrics. I had decided to make Eleanor Branson a quilt. After my chores were done I pulled out the pattern and my rotary cutter. I didn't have my machines set up yet, but the cutting table was there, waiting for me. Quilting was soothing, I was looking forward to a respite from my twirling thoughts.

But today I had trouble concentrating. I kept thinking about Lynda and wondering what she was doing at the dog track. Cutting fabric today would probably be a mistake. I would just iron the fabric, that was pretty simple to do.

As the steam hissed up from my ironing board I watched the wrinkles disappear and the fabric smooth out. But, this required no real concentration and I found my thoughts back at the Greyhound Park.

Dog track. Dogs. Suddenly I knew how the drugs were being moved. Heart pounding, I went to the phone. Damn! Rick wasn't home. Then I remembered. He had planned to help a buddy move to Moses Lake. He wouldn't be back until late Sunday night.

I was going to have to wait.

CHAPTER 32

▼

By the time I got to work Monday morning I was sure had I had figured out how the drug scheme worked. I had hoped to talk to Rick Sunday night, but he must have gotten in too late to call me. I was dying to talk to him, but Rick had patients to see and I had work to do. We knew it would raise questions if we tried to talk privately at work and that was something we both wanted to avoid. Lunch time would be our best bet.

Finally it was noon. Brad and Lynda went out to eat, but I still felt nervous talking to Rick about my ideas inside the building. I led him outside with our sandwiches.

I had the stack of copied disks from my hiding place and added the one I'd retrieved on Friday to the pile.

"I think I figured out what Lynda's doing," I told him, "But first I want to talk about these." I handed him the disks. "Go see your friend the deputy again. Ask him if he can run them in their computer lab. Maybe the proof they need is on them somewhere and we won't have to play detective any more. I don't know if my nerves can take it."

"I thought you looked a little rattled this morning. Is what happened on Friday still bugging you?"

"No, it's what I think I figured out over the weekend. Saturday I went to the Factory Outlet Mall to get a winter coat. Since the Greyhound Park was so close, I decided to go over there. I've been thinking about getting a dog and wanted some information on their Greyhound adoption program. Lynda was there, in a meeting with somebody. I didn't actually see her, but I heard her voice."

"Lynda was at the Greyhound track? What was she doing there?"

"She was in a meeting with someone and I heard her saying something about needing another matched dozen soon."

"Dozen what?"

"Dogs, Rick. This has been churning around in my head all weekend. You know how when you take a dog across the border into Mexico you have to have papers for it—we already talked about that. The papers describe the dog, so that you can't bring over different dogs at different times with just one set of papers.

"Here's what I think Lynda is doing. She arranges to have Greyhounds 'adopted' by people in those four states that we have noticed the boxes coming from. There must be somebody at the track involved too, providing the dogs. Those people obtain health certificates from their vets. They take the dogs one at a time across the border, feed them balloons of cocaine or whatever and bring them back to the US. Then, I think they slaughter them and send the bodies to Lynda. She retrieves the drugs, puts it in urns and ships it off, just like we'd already figured out."

"Yeah, but we already talked about that. Wouldn't the border patrol guys wonder about somebody coming through all the time with a different dog?" Rick asked.

"That must be why I heard her ask the man at the track about a matched dozen," I said. "They're careful to use dogs that look the same so the people who're taking the dogs back and forth across the border don't have to get new health certificates all the time and the border guards wouldn't get suspicious. These people must have some sort of legitimate reason to be going in and out of Mexico all the time, too."

Rick stared at me. "How diabolical," he said. "That sounds like it'd work, all right, and she'd be smart enough to pull it off. Lynda must charge the smugglers a fee for each dog then she gets paid for sending the drugs on. I bet you're right about the guy at the track being involved, too. He would almost have to be, if he's supplying identical dogs by the dozen." Rick glanced at his watch. "Brad and Lynda'll be back any minute. We'd better go in. I'll take these discs to my neighbor, Tom, and have him take a look at them."

I was glad the next few clinic days were busy. It was no problem to act natural around the clients and their pets, but tough around Lynda. I kept thinking about the boy that had died from drugs she probably sent to his town and about all the dogs that were being butchered.

Rick and I had plans for dinner on Friday. I hoped he'd have some news by then.

CHAPTER 33

▼

Rick and I were starting to get paranoid. The thought of attracting attention from drug dealers had me scared to death. Afraid of being overheard in a restaurant, we decided to get take-and-bake pizzas and eat at my house Friday night.

"Did you get a chance to talk to Tom?" I asked Rick while I liked the pepperoni grease off my fingers.

"Yeah, I did. He asked me if he could tell our story to one of the detectives. I told him that would be great. I went ahead and told him to have the guy come by here tonight. His name is Martin Adams."

"I'm really glad you did that. Maybe now we can make get someplace with this."

Detective Martin Adams turned out to be a nondescript man in his late forties. He listened without interrupting to Rick's and my suspicions.

When we were done he said, "I'm going to tell you two some things, but you have to keep them quiet. Can you do that?" We both nodded. "We know there's drugs running through the Spokane area, but we haven't been able to pin them down. There've been several arrests made in outlying areas and nearby states and they've all said the stuff came from Spokane. Trouble is, none of it is being sold here, so our usual information sources haven't been much help. These people are clever. If they're using dogs like you think they are it's a new method." He stopped and looked at us. "How involved do you two want to be in this deal?"

Rick said, "I'd like to stop Lynda, if she is doing this. Someday I hope the clinic will be mine and I don't want to see it destroyed."

"I want to help too," I said. "I read about a boy that died from an overdose then I had a real vivid dream about a kid who was begging me for help. I'd do whatever I could to prevent any more deaths. I feel bad about all the dogs, too."

"Tell us what we can do, Detective Adams," said Rick.

"Okay. Please call me Marty. Now, what we're going to need is proof, real, hard evidence. Without probable cause we can't search the clinic or any packages going in or out. But, if either one of you could divert one of those boxes and open it, then all you'd have to do is call and report the fact that you think you've found drugs. That would give us our probable cause."

"That's what we've been trying to do," I said. "Wasn't there anything on those disks?"

"Well, there was lots of information. Now we know what and where *something* is coming from and going to. We have lots of names, but it turns out that all the addresses are false though, so that's a bit of a dead end. But, there's nothing on those disks that actually mentions drugs. That's why we need to get a hold of one of those boxes."

Rick and I looked at each other. "The only problem, Marty," Rick said, "Is that Lynda keeps a really close watch on the comings and goings of her boxes. Plus, when she's working in the back she always locks herself in. It's going to be really tough to catch her doing anything."

"Is there any way to intercept one of the boxes while they're in the UPS truck?" I asked.

Marty shrugged, "Sure, Maggie. But, we're still limited by a lack of probable cause. We need a damn good reason to search a UPS truck. Right now we don't have one. And you know that if we search and find something without a proper search warrant, well, any half-way competent lawyer would get the evidence tossed."

"It keeps coming back to what Rick and I might be able to do at the clinic, doesn't it?"

Marty nodded. "That's about it, yes." He paused for a minute. "Do you think Dr. Mancusco is involved too?"

Rick shook his head. "I'd be really surprised if he is. He seems content to let Lynda handle everything connected with the crematory and cemetery. The most he ever does is talk to a client who's lost an animal about the services we offer or show somebody a cemetery plot. Brad's such a straight arrow that I don't think even the promise of big money would seduce him."

"Do you think he'd be willing to help us?" Marty said.

Rick shook his head again. "He'd be more apt to confront Lynda immediately and then God knows what might happen. She's so greedy I wouldn't put it past her to kill him to save her business. I think Maggie and I are all you have."

Great. Here I had thought that getting Phil and his murderous buddies out of my life would insure my safety. Now I'm going to deliberately put myself in harm's way? Oh, well, I've always said there are two kinds of people when it comes to trouble, those who jump away from it and those who jump toward it. I wanted to be a jump-away person, but it was too late to consider that. I had already made the leap.

Marty stood up and walked to the door. "Okay. I've got to get going. Let me know if there's anything I can help you with. Like if you think you can get Lynda to talk I could get you a body wire, that kind of thing."

"Thanks, Marty. We'll let you know," said Rick.

Rick closed the door behind Marty and turned to me. "Let's take a glass of wine out to the hot tub. Maybe the combination of alcohol and hot water will stimulate our brains."

I was already in the water by the time Rick came out. I knew he didn't have the time to get to the gym, but wrestling around with nervous horses and cranky cattle had worked better than any Nautilus machine. His chest was broad, tapering into a flat stomach where I could see muscles move as he walked. I felt my own stomach tighten watching the muscles in his arms flex as he maneuvered his way into the water.

The crisp night was perfect for hot tub soaking. We sat without talking for a few minutes, trying to unwind from the evening.

Rick spoke first. "So, any ideas?"

I shook my head. From the corner of my eye I could see Henry. He was sitting on one of the cat tree's upper perches in the kennel. He was watching us intently. "No, nothing specific. I can't see any way to get hold of a box that has been delivered and getting hold of one that's going out would be nearly impossible. I keep coming back to the idea that one of us has to somehow get into the back when Lynda's working and get a hold of a baggie of drugs. That is, if our suspicions are correct."

"Meow. Meow! MEOW!"

Henry was standing on his hind legs with his front paws on the side of the kennel. He was bobbing his head up and down with each meow.

"Henry seems to agree," said Rick. "I do too. The trouble is, I can't think of how to get back there while she's working. It'd have to be at just the right time."

"Timing seems to be the whole problem," I said. "If we knew exactly when she started work after a delivery, or if we knew when UPS was coming, we could maybe manage to snag something. They don't even come on the same *day* each week, much less the same time. And neither one of us can just hang out and wait without making her wonder what we're doing. This is going to make me crazy. To have this going on right under our noses and not be able to *do* anything about it."

"I know what you mean. Well, I'd better get home." Rick stepped out of the hot tub to give me a hand out and draped my bathrobe over my shoulders. "We'll have to watch for an opening of any sort. I'll talk to you tomorrow, okay?"

He put his arms around me and kissed me gently. As my knees threatened to buckle, he let me go. I watched him walk across the deck and into the house to get dressed. Within minutes he was waving to me from his car.

For a few more minutes I stood and looked at the stars, willing the fluttering that went from my throat down to my nether regions to settle down. Then I went in and went to bed.

CHAPTER 34

▼

I spent the weekend putting together the rest of my quilting studio, as I was going to call the shop. A 20x30 building was too big to be called a sewing room and I hoped to start doing some quilting work for others, too, so a studio it would be.

The sewing part of the room was simple to set up. The legs on the sewing table unfolded and my trusty little Viking, almost 15 years old now, slid into place. I had all my small sewing supplies in portable plastic drawer units that had been moved as is. Other than some of the drawers being a bit jumbled up they were all ready to go—I just assigned them their places.

The quilting machine was another matter, though. It took me a while longer to put together as it had been several years since I used it. Phil had not been interested in my having a space where it would fit, and I had to study the pieces before I could remember how it all went together.

The table itself was 14 feet long, but only about two feet wide from front to back. The legs and upper supports for the rollers were each just one piece. I was gratified to see that all the bolts and nuts that were needed to attach the ends to the table were still there. With any luck I'd be able to do this without a trip to the hardware store. I dug out a crescent wrench and went to work.

With the table assembled, the only thing left to do was put the sewing machine itself on its tracks. I added oil to all the oil ports. I would let it seep down into the gears before I tried to run it. It had sat for a long time and was probably dry inside.

The setup done, I stepped back to look. Wow. I had forgotten what an impressive sight this Noltings Longarm Quilting Machine was. I hoped my quilting skills hadn't gotten too rusty. At least I still knew how it worked, that was easy. Or it sounded easy.

When a customer brought me a finished quilt top I assembled it with batting and the fabric the person wanted to use for the back. These three layers I spread out on my pinning table and pinned them together from the top. Then, I took the quilt to the longarm machine. The longarm table had two rollers, each with a wide piece of canvas attached along the length of the roller. One edge of the quilt was pinned to this canvas. The quilt was then rolled up on the roller, and the opposite edge was pinned to the canvas on the other roller. Using a ratchet-like handle, the rollers were turned until the quilt was taut between them. On the ends of the machine were two clamps fastened onto long lengths of the loop side of Velcro fastening tape. These clamps were fixed to the ends of the quilt and also pulled taut, then secured to the ends of the table where the hook side of the Velcro tape had been fastened.

Once this was done, quilting could begin. On a regular sewing machine, the fabric is moved under the needle as it goes up and down, stitching. A longarm quilting machine was the opposite. The fabric, the quilt, was held still while the sewing machine was moved over the quilt, stitching all the while. The instructions that came with the machine when I bought it had not been terribly helpful, merely describing machine quilting as a form of "dancing with the machine." But, those instructions had also said it could ten hours to pick out what was wrongly stitched in ten seconds, and I believed it.

There were two handles just above the needle on the sewing machine part. I used these handles to "drive" the sewing head around on the quilt. Sometimes I would do freehand designs, other times I had to trace the pattern on using a stencil, or draw guidelines on the quilt top with a piece of chalk. It was both fun and frustrating work. Fun when the machine ran well and the pattern flowed, frustrating when thread broke repeatedly and the design was tough.

I was excited to get things set up, though. I would need to do some practicing before I put my business cards out at the local fabric and quilting stores.

Now that the room was ready, I felt that familiar itch. I needed to make a quilt. I would wait a bit on Eleanor's. I just wasn't quite ready to dive into a tough project with so much else going on. So, I decided to make one of my instant gratification quilts, what I like to call a hobo quilt, as it had a ruffled, sort of ragged, soft look about it.

It had been so long since I looked at my stash of fabrics I had forgotten all the wonderful pieces I had. It did not take me long to select a bunch of different colors and patterns of flannel, this would really be a snuggly quilt.

I spent the rest of the day cutting and sewing. By dinnertime I had all the squares finished. All that remained was assembling the squares into strips, then the strips into the quilt. Some clipping of the exposed seam allowances and a trip through the washer and dryer to fluff and ruffle whose clipped edges would finish the project.*

When I finally creaked to my feet to go find something to eat, I was tired, but happy. I stood at the door of my new quilting studio, hand on the light switch. "What a killer quilt studio you are," I told the empty room. "Hey, that's it! I'll call my business Killer Quilts!"

* Instructions for making a Hobo quilt can be found at the end of this book

CHAPTER 35

▼

Before I knew it, it was Monday morning. Because I had managed to stay busy all weekend, I had almost forgotten about drugs and dead dogs. But now it was right back in the front of my thoughts again.

Henry was sitting by his carrier. As usual he was eager to go to work with me. Cleo, secure in the knowledge that she wasn't leaving home, was now able to come out and watch us leave. I knew she got lonely during the day because when I got home in the evenings the evidence was everywhere: unrolled toilet paper and other messes created by a bored cat. I was beginning to think I was going to have to get another cat for company for her or start leaving Henry home. But, he seemed to like going with me so much. Besides, if I'm able to get hold of any proof I can use his carrier again to get it out of the building, I thought. Its coming and going with me was so routine now I didn't think anybody paid any attention to it anymore.

There was a thin column of steam rising from the crematory stack. Lynda must be at work early.

Inside, the clinic looked the same as it always had. But, the thought that this might actually be a link in a drug network gave everything a sinister cast. I shivered. I hope we can get this sorted out pretty soon, I thought.

A client dragging a large terrified dog distracted me; the day had begun.

I looked up at the clock, surprised. The morning was gone. I reached out to switch the phone to the answering machine for the lunch hour and jumped when it rang under my hand.

"Hi, Maggie, it's Georgia. I'm sorry to bother you at work, but I have a problem. How would you like another cat?"

"Hi, Georgia. It's good to hear from you. Another cat? What do you mean?"

"This morning when I went to get some wood for the stove I found a kitten. It's just a tiny thing, fluffy and orange-colored. I think it's a female, but I'm not sure. The poor thing is a mess. Her fur is full of mats and her nose is running. I think she's about starved to death, too—when I picked her up it was like I had hold of a handful of feathers. She was able to eat an egg yolk mixed with a little milk, though, and then she fell asleep. What do you think? Can you take her?"

"It's kind of funny, Georgia. I was just thinking this morning that I need a cat to keep Cleo company because Henry comes to work with me almost every day. Sounds like this baby needs some vet attention, too. Is there any way you could bring her to the clinic? I'm sure Brad or Rick would be happy to take a look at her."

"I was hoping you'd say that. My cat is having quite a snit-fit. I'm afraid he'd make short work of this little thing if he could get a hold of her. Sure. I can come by. When would be a good time?"

What a pathetic scrap of fur this kitten was. Even though Georgia had cut away most of the mats and wiped it down with a damp cloth, its fur was still filthy. Not only was its nose running, but also its eyes. The insides of its ears were black, probably ear mites, I thought, and its stomach was bloated. Add worms to the list. It was a female, and looked very young to me.

"It's a good thing your friend found her today," said Brad. "She probably would not have survived the night. She may not make it even so—she's pretty sick."

Brad gave her an antibiotic shot for the obvious upper respiratory infection, cleaned out her ears, gave her a dose of worm medicine, and cleaned the crusts away from her eyes and nostrils.

"Let's keep her here tonight, Maggie. I'm going to be coming in a couple of times to see to Frank Beeson's dog, so I can check on her."

"Thanks, Brad. That sounds like a good idea. Tomorrow I'll bring the other carrier so I can take her home when she's ready."

"I hope she makes it," he said. "She's going to be a pretty cat if she does."

Henry had followed us into the exam room. He reached out with a careful paw and touched the kitten. Then he sniffed her all over. He made a distasteful face at the smells of all the medications, but licked her between the ears anyway. Brad smiled at a tiny buzz-saw sound. "She's well enough to purr, anyway."

Even though I came early the next morning, Brad had gotten to the clinic before me. He was standing in front of the kitten's cage when I walked into the back. Afraid to look, I stopped just inside the door and said, "Well?"

"See for yourself." Brad stepped away from the cage.

Although still ratty-looking, the kitten was very much alive. She was sitting in the middle of her blanket washing her face. Sick cats don't bathe, so I was thrilled to see that.

"She just finished a couple of tablespoons of Gerber Junior Chicken then used her litter pan. We got lucky, Maggie. I think she's going to make it."

"What a tiny thing she is. What do you think, Brad, twelve weeks old?"

"Twelve weeks would be about the maximum. I'd say she's more like eight to ten weeks. Hard to figure a kitten this young being out on her own. I wonder if she was dumped by someone or the only survivor of a litter? No way to know."

"She's going to be a real dark orange isn't she? I think I'll call her Marmalade," I told him. "If you think it's okay, I'll take her home."

"Sure. She'll need some coddling now is all. Introduce her slowly to regular cat food—continue with the baby food meats for a few days then start gradually mixing in canned cat food. You'll have to clean her ears out with Mitox a couple of times a day for a week or so until those mites are gone, and give her Amoxi-drops too. The worm medicine shouldn't have to be repeated, but you'll need to keep an eye on her stools for a few days anyway."

Cleo's carrier was deemed acceptable and the kitten rode home with scarcely a squeak. I settled her in the spare bedroom with a cozy nest box and food and water.

All was quiet overnight and by noon the next day Marmalade looked even better. She was eating and drinking without any problems and had cleaned all the dirt from her fur. I decided to bring her out of the bedroom and see what Cleo and Henry would do.

For safety's sake, in case Henry and Cleo reacted badly, I put Marmalade back in the carrier. I set it on the floor in the living room, but did not open the door. Although she was small, Cleo could turn into a Tazmanian Devil—twirling in a jealous rage. I wanted Marmalade's first introduction to her new family members to take place behind the protection of a wire door.

Cleo surprised me. I accepted some yowling and spitting, but instead all she showed was intense interest. Henry had already met the kitten at the clinic, so he just sat and watched Cleo. I took a deep breath and opened the carrier door. Cautiously Marmalade stepped out. Cleo and Henry both walked over to her. She stood rock still, waiting. Each cat sniffed her thoroughly. As he had at the clinic, Henry licked her. Soon Cleo did too. Marmalade then had a bath she'd probably never forget. Cleo and Henry each went over one of Marmalade's sides then they traded places and washed the other one. When they were done they walked off, Henry looking back at her as if to say, "Well, you coming?" Still wobbly from illness and starvation, Marmalade tottered after them. I realized I'd been holding my breath and let it out with a sigh.

"Whew. I didn't know if that was going to work out," I said. "I'm sure glad it did."

CHAPTER 36

▼

That night I slept alone. Usually Cleo was by my feet and Henry spent the night at my shoulder with his head on a pillow. I put the nest box I had fixed for Marmalade in the corner of my room. At midnight an owl hooting outside woke me up. I got up and looked out the window then turned to check on Marmalade.

Cleo and Henry were curled up asleep on their sides in Marmalade's box, facing each other. In between them Marmalade nestled—warm, safe and sound asleep. Delighted, I went back to bed and slept too.

Henry and Cleo scarcely left Marmalade's side all day Tuesday. I wasn't sure if they loved her or just didn't trust her, but either way they were all getting along.

I spent the day finishing my hobo quilt. The rich colors I had picked out looked wonderful on my bed. I could hardly wait to crawl under it.

The next morning I expected Henry to be too busy with Marmalade to want to come with me. But, by the time I was ready to leave he was sitting by his carrier with an "Okay, Mom, let's go," expression.

I was first to arrive at the clinic. Brad was taking the day off and Rick must have gotten an early call. Lynda, after several early-morning trips to open the door, had reluctantly given me the security code again. I unlocked the door and punched in the numbers.

The morning wasn't heavily booked for a change. The first patients I was able to take care of myself. Rick came in the door as the last one left before an empty half an hour in the schedule.

"Now you get back! What'd you do, wait out on the road until you knew it was safe to come in?"

"Sure, he said. "I'm not so dumb, after all. How'd the kitten do?"

"Really well. Cleo and Henry adopted her like she was their own. I'd been worried about what Cleo would do. Henry was about six months old when I brought him home and she was very upset, doing a very credible imitation of a Tasmanian devil. Even though she had no kittens and would never be having any kittens, she just knew this male interloper would have to be destroyed before he could hurt the kittens. He still is about half afraid of her when she gets wound up. This kitten being female she represented less of a threat, I guess. They slept together in a puddle of cats all night."

"That's good." Rick went over to Henry and scratched him behind the ears. "Look," he said, pointing out the window. "Here come some more." I saw the UPS truck pull in. This time there were six large boxes.

"This might be our chance," said Rick, loading the first box onto the hand truck. "Let's take these in the back. As soon as I take a look at the dog I spayed yesterday I'll put one of the boxes in one of the kennels with the solid doors. Later I can come back and pick it up. If this is going to work we'll have to take the whole box and open it someplace else. Lynda has to think that it never got here."

"Okay. I hope you have better luck than the day I tried it to look at one. Why don't you just put five on the hand truck. I'll take those to the back and park them by the crematory door and you can go ahead and put away the one we're going to keep."

With Henry at my heels I maneuvered the hand truck down the hall to the crematory door. I set the pile down and pulled the hand truck away. I turned to go.

"Thanks, Maggie."

I jumped like I'd been shot. "Lynda! Good Lord, you scared me to death. I thought you were taking the day off too. How'd you get here? Where's your car?"

Lynda was standing in the doorway, laughing. "Ha! You should see your face. White as a sheet! Brad dropped me off. I knew these boxes would be coming this morning and I wanted to take care of them right away. They start getting ripe pretty fast. Here, help me bring 'em in." She pushed the door open wider. I slid the boxes back onto the hand truck and rolled it through the door. Lynda had me take them into her preparation room. I hoped for a chance to look around a little, but she hurried me back out. I put the hand truck away and went to my desk. Rick was walking past me carrying the sixth box.

"Lynda's here," I hissed at him. He nodded and kept on going.

I heard him rapping at the crematory door. "Lynda? The UPS guy forgot one of your boxes, open the door and I'll bring it in for you."

I sat at my desk and waited for Rick to come back. I could hear doors opening and closing and the faint mumble of voices. Lynda sounded like she always did; Rick and I had been lucky again.

"That was close," Rick said, coming back out in the waiting room.

"You're telling me. She almost scared me silly. I had no idea she was here. Thank God she didn't hear us talking," I whispered. "Are we ever going to get a chance to get a hold of one of those boxes?"

"Yeah, probably when we least expect it. We'll just have to be ready when that time comes."

A man came in with a limping dog and Rick took them into an exam room. That was the last patient before lunch. I fled out the door and went to the McDonald's on Sullivan to eat. I needed some distance from Lynda.

It was close to the end of the day when I realized I hadn't seen Henry since morning. I searched and called, but was unable to find him. I knocked on the crematory door.

"Lynda? Are you still here?"

"Yes, Maggie. What do you want?"

"I can't find Henry anywhere. Is it possible he slipped in there when we had the door open earlier?"

"I haven't seen him and I doubt if he'd stay in here willingly. He doesn't seem to like me very much."

"Can I come in and look for him, please?"

Linda opened the door. "No, I'd rather you didn't. Just stand there and call him. If he's in here, which I doubt, he'll come to you, won't he?"

"I hope so. But, he's never been back here so he might be too scared to try and get out. How about if you prop the door open for a few minutes? If neither of us is around he's more apt to come out. I'll call him from the front."

"Well, okay, but I still don't think he's in here."

Back at the front desk I picked up Henry's carrier and rattled the door and called his name. Usually this brought him running—he knew it was time to go. Fifteen minutes passed. No Henry. I was starting to get seriously worried when I heard a shout from the back. I headed in that direction when I was startled by a black streak zooming by me. With a thump Henry landed on the front counter. He sat down and started to wash his hind foot.

I left him there and went to see what the shouting was all about. Lynda was in the process of locking the crematory door.

"I guess we're even now, Maggie. That cat of yours scared me about like I did you earlier. He must have been hiding under one of the sinks. I leaned down to pick up a towel I dropped when he ran out across my hand. I ended up on my rear on the floor. All I saw was his tail going out the door."

"I'm sorry, Lynda. He usually doesn't come back here with me. I guess his curiosity got the better of him today." I struggled not to laugh. I'd have given a lot to see her flat on her butt on the floor.

Henry was sitting in his carrier—he was ready to go home. "You bad boy. You scared Lynda."

"Meow!" he said, bobbing his head up and down.

CHAPTER 37

▼

On Friday I watched, frustrated, as the UPS man took away six boxes of urns. At this rate there'd never be anything to call Marty about.

By the time I went home that evening my frustration had not abated. As I unlocked my front door I could hear the phone start to ring.

I picked up the receiver. "Hello?"

"Is this Maggie Jackson?"

"Yes, may I help you?"

"Yeah. This is Phyllis at the Post Falls Greyhound Track. You had filled out an application for a dog? We have some available now if you're still interested."

"Oh, yes. I'd nearly forgotten. How does this work?"

"What we like to do is set up an appointment with you to come out and see the dogs. You pick the one you like and if the two of you get along you take it home on a trial basis. If things go well we send you the papers. If it doesn't work out you can call and make arrangements to bring it back."

"I have a friend who's a veterinarian. Can he come with me?"

"Sure, bring anybody you like. Now, when do you want to come out?"

"How about tomorrow, around one? If that's not okay with my friend I'll call you this afternoon."

"That'll be fine. Clyde handles our adoptions. You can plan on meeting him in the lobby if I don't hear back from you."

I broke the connection and called Rick.

"So, I'm glad I got the call here instead of at the clinic," I finished. "I don't really want Lynda to know I've had any contact with the dog track. I have an appointment to go see some dogs tomorrow afternoon at one. You want to come? You can do a health check on the dog and maybe we can pick up something about our drug smuggling theory while we're there."

"Sure, that'd be fine. Do you want to have lunch at Applebee's first?"

"Okay, I love the food there. Why don't I drive? If I end up bringing a dog home I want him or her to acclimate to my stuff first. Should I pick you up about 11:30?"

"Sounds good. I saw those six boxes go out this morning. It looks like Lynda is getting busier."

"I wish we'd been able to get a hold of one of them. I almost got into the back on Wednesday, though. When I helped Lynda move the boxes in Henry must have slipped in when we weren't looking. He was there all afternoon. It'd be nice if he could talk—I bet he saw a lot."

"Sometimes it seems like he can," Rick said.

"Yeah, I know. But, I don't think Detective Adams would accept meows and head bobs as enough to establish probable cause."

Saturday afternoon after lunch Rick and I drove to the dog track. A man met us in the lobby.

"Are you Maggie? I'm Clyde. You're here to see some dogs, right?"

"Yes. This is Dr. Evans, he's a friend of mine from the vet clinic where I work."

"Nice to meet you both. Let me lock up my office and I'll take you back to the adoption kennels." He walked over and locked the door of the office where I had heard Lynda's voice the last time I had been there. I tipped my head and bugged my eyes at Rick, trying to tell him about that office. He looked at me oddly and shook his head, obviously my body language was inadequate.

"Okay," Clyde said, "Let's go." He took us through a door in the back wall. We walked into a large room with a dozen roomy kennels on each side. He led us over to the right side and pointed at the cages.

"The four dogs on this side are the ones that are available. Go ahead and take a look. You can open the doors and let 'em out if you want. Even though they're really mellow dogs we keep 'em muzzled for safety."

"Oh, Rick," I said, "Aren't they gorgeous?"

The dogs were different colors and all females. Two were a dark gray, one a soft tan, and the fourth a black and tan brindle. Rick opened the kennel doors and the dogs came out. I sat down on the floor. The gray and tan dogs were calm and accepting of my attentions, but held themselves aloof. The brindle came over

to me and lay down, putting her head on my knee and gazing up at me out of liq-
uid brown eyes. She would be the one, I knew. I stood up. The dog stood by my
leg and when I moved she moved too. I looked across the room and saw that all
the kennels on that side seemed to be filled with fawn-colored dogs. "What about
these?" I asked, walking over for a closer look.

"Those have all been adopted out," Clyde said, steering me back to the other
side of the room. "I think this brindle bitch likes you—that's the one you should
take."

"But I like the lighter colored ones..."

"I said those are taken! Now, if you want a dog it has to be one of these four. I
need to go up front for a minute. Spend some more time with the dogs. I'll be
right back."

Rick was on his knees running his hands along the brindle's sides and looking
at her teeth and eyes. "As far as I can tell without doing any lab work, she's
healthy. She seems to be a nice dog too."

I was scarcely listening. "Rick! I bet those are the dogs that Lynda was talking
about that day. Did you see how nervous Clyde got when I went over to look at
them? I wish I knew why he left in such a hurry."

Rick walked over and looked at the dogs. "Well, they are pretty much identical. You could be right."

Clyde burst through the door and grabbed Rick by the arm. He pulled him
back over to where I was standing. "I said get away from those dogs."

"What's the big deal? I was only looking at them."

"They've been a little sick. I didn't want you to bring any germs over to these
dogs. Ms. Jackson? I don't have all day. Have you decided?"

"Yes. I'll take the brindle one. She seems healthy and friendly."

Clyde grabbed the leash I had taken out of my purse and clipped it to the
dog's collar. I got the feeling he would bodily carry us off the premises if he
thought he could get away with it. He rushed us out the door. "You have thirty
days to decide. If we don't hear from you by the end of that time, we'll send you
the papers. After that she's your responsibility."

By now we were standing in the parking lot. I opened my car door and the
dog hopped willingly into the back seat and lay down with a sigh. Clyde held out
a clipboard. "Sign here that you're taking this dog. Like I said, if we don't here
from you in thirty days we'll send you her papers. Hope you enjoy your dog.
Good-bye." He turned and hurried off.

We got in the Blazer and I reached in to the back seat and took the muzzle off the dog. "I wonder if Clyde meant to leave this on. It seems we really rattled him, doesn't it."

"Yeah," said Rick, "And I wonder why. I don't think we asked any pointed questions, do you?"

"No, but if those are the 'drug dogs' maybe our looking at them was enough to unnerve him. You know what else? He could have been the guy that called to talk to Lynda the day I copied the disks. That guy's name was Clyde. Maybe he recognized my voice or something."

"And another thing," said Rick, "He probably went up front and looked me up in the phone book when you told him I was a vet and mentioned that you worked at the same clinic I do. He'd have found me listed with Brad in the clinic's ad. Probably scared the pee out of him."

I couldn't help but laugh. "Serves him right, the creep. Hope he has a change of underwear in his office." My new pet had stretched out full length on the back seat and was sound asleep. "Look at her, Rick, isn't she beautiful? I bet anything that's what those other dogs are for. It really makes me angry that people would kill them to smuggle drugs. We *have* to get a hold of some proof for Marty!" I threw the muzzle out the window onto the ground and we pulled out of the parking lot, headed for home.

CHAPTER 38

▼

The rest of the weekend flew by. After some initial back-arching and tail-puffing, all three cats began to accept the presence of a dog. Predictably, Henry was the first to calm down. Once he realized the dog was not going to chase him, he relaxed; even to the point of curling up next to her while she napped on the hearth rug. The dog spent the rest of Saturday and all day Sunday exploring the house and yard. Even though she could stand on her hind legs with her front paws almost to the top of the fence, she seemed to have no desire to try and jump over. No doubt those strands of barbed wire that kept the deer out would also keep her in. She was also content to sleep either on the floor by my bed or in the living room. Now I was trying to come up with a name that fit her.

"I thought of 'Brandy'," I told Rick Monday morning, "For some reason that brindle coat reminds me of the color of brandy. I'm not sure, though. Maybe I'll wait until I see more of her personality for an inspiration."

"I thought you were calling her Marmalade," said Lynda from her office door.

"Oh, that's what I named the kitten. I ended up getting a dog this weekend."

"A dog? What did you get?"

I looked at Rick. He shrugged slightly. "I, uh, got a Greyhound."

"A Greyhound? Where did you find one?"

"Through the adoption program at the dog track."

By now Lynda was standing in front of me. "When did you go there?" She was watching my face intently.

"Oh, it was awhile ago, on a day when I was shopping for a winter coat. I don't remember exactly." I shrugged, trying to appear casual, though I could feel my insides doing back flips. "I was at the Outlet Mall and decided to run over to the Greyhound Park. I'd been thinking about getting a dog and had heard about their adoption program. I filled out an application and they called me last week to come see some available dogs. Why?"

Her face relaxed. "Oh, no reason. I just wondered." Her office phone rang and she went to answer it.

Rick looked at me and nodded. I understood. Her behavior was enough to tell us that we must be right—those twelve dogs we saw *were* destined to be sacrificed to the drug trade.

Lynda's phone rang steadily all day. She made several trips into the back and I could hear her slamming things around and muttering. A few minutes before closing time she came up to my desk.

Her hair stuck out from her head where she'd been raking her fingers through it and the knees of her slacks were dirty, like she'd been crawling around on the floor.

"You haven't found anything you couldn't identify lying around on the floor or anywhere have you?"

"Like what?"

"Oh, sort of a funny-looking, blue, balloon-like thing?"

"No. What on earth would that be?"

She wiped her face and her hand came away wet—she was dripping sweat.

"The owners of one of those dogs that came in last week supposedly had some sort of amulet thing tied around the dog's neck. They wanted it put on the front of the urn. They had stuffed it into a blue condom, of all things, to keep it dry."

"No, I haven't seen anything like that."

"Are you positive? These people are going bananas. They've called me about ten times today."

"I'm sure that'd be something I'd remember. Why is this thing so important, anyway?"

"They belong to what sounds to me like an odd religious cult. This amulet is important to insure the dog's entry into heaven or something. It doesn't make any sense to me, but that's not important. What's important is that it matters to them. Do you think that cat of yours could have carried it off?"

"He could have, but he usually brings me anything he finds and there hasn't been anything like that."

"Well, we're going to have to search the whole building just in case. These people are threatening to sue us. I need you to come in tomorrow and help us." Lynda turned and stomped away.

The next day we spent going over every inch of the building. Lynda had Rick go in the back with her to search, she assigned me the front of the building. Henry found the process fascinating. He followed me everywhere and I frequently had to push his black nose out of my face so I could see what I was doing. We found nothing that looked like Lynda's missing "blue condom." She was on the phone in her office when I got ready to leave that evening.

"Yes, I'm concerned too," I heard her say. "Isn't it possible that it never was here at all?" She paused, probably listening, I thought.

"You know there's never been a problem before at this end and there isn't one now. It didn't get here. That's all I can tell you."

I heard her get up from her desk. I busied myself securing the latch on Henry's carrier. Lynda didn't come out, but shut her door.

Her voice was now too muffled to understand. I picked up Henry and went home.

As soon as I got there I called Rick. "Are you thinking what I'm thinking?" I asked him. "That Lynda has somehow lost a baggie of cocaine or whatever?"

"Yes, that's *exactly* what I've been thinking. Could Henry really have carried one away with him? We both know how he likes to pack things around."

"Yeah, but like I told Lynda, he usually brings things he finds to me making that odd moaning and snarking noise he uses when he "kills" something. He likes me to make a big deal over it and praise him. He hasn't brought me anything for awhile though, other than the usual bits of crumpled paper he digs out of the waste basket. Did you get a chance to see anything interesting when you were in the back helping her search?"

"No, she keeps things pretty neat. I still bet Henry somehow got away with the 'amulet in the blue condom' Lynda's looking for."

"It's a reasonable assumption except for one thing. If he did carry it off, where did he put it? We were over that whole building with a fine-toothed comb."

Rick sighed, "I know. It'd sure be great if either you or I could find it. That'd be our probable cause for Marty Adams."

"Maybe Henry has a hidey-hole we haven't found. He could bring something out to me yet. We'll have to wait and see, I guess."

CHAPTER 39

▼

Wednesday started out like any other day. The usual parade of animals came through the waiting room, Henry sat on the counter greeting everybody and the phone was busy. I was only half-aware of the phone ringing unanswered in Lynda's office.

Brad came out front midway through the lunch break. "Maggie, have you seen Lynda today?" When I shook my head he frowned, "I hope she's all right. She came home late last night and was gone by the time I got up this morning. I can't imagine where she is or what she could be doing."

I can, I thought, but I didn't say anything.

We both looked up at the sound of the front door opening. It was Lynda. She walked in with her head down.

"Lynda!" Brad said. He went to her and put his arms around her.

She pushed him away, "Careful. I have a couple of broken ribs."

"Broken ribs? From what? Where were you last night and this morning? I've been worried sick."

"Oh, it was really stupid," she said. "I went out to the cemetery after I left here yesterday and I tripped and fell onto a pile of rocks. I must have knocked myself out, because the next thing I knew it was dark. It's all sort of fuzzy, but I must have driven home. I didn't want to disturb you, so I just lay down on the sofa to sleep. Then this morning I woke up and I couldn't breathe very well. I didn't want to wake you, so I went to the hospital. They did x-rays and taped me up." She lifted her head.

I gasped. Her left eye was swollen nearly shut. The puffy flesh around it was stained a deep purple.

"I guess I hit my eye when I fell, too," she said, smiling weakly.

"You should be home," I said. "You probably have a concussion."

"Yes, please, go home," said Brad. "We can handle things here."

"No, I'm all right. I'm expecting a shipment today that I need to take care of. I'll be fine. My head's okay, it's the ribs that hurt."

She went in her office and shut the door.

Brad stood for a minute looking at the closed door. "I don't know..." he muttered. He turned to me. "If Lynda fell and hit her face hard enough on a pile of rocks like to blacken her eye like that don't you think there'd be some other marks, too?"

"Not necessarily, depending on how she landed. Why?"

"Oh, I don't know. It's just that she's been acting kind of funny for several months now." He must have noticed my expression, as he went on, "It's nothing you'd notice, because it started before you came to work here. For some reason Lynda was highly suspicious of the last front office woman, Sandra. She would never tell me exactly what bothered her, she just called it a 'feeling' she had. As you know, eventually Sandra quit, just walked out one day and didn't come back. I think Lynda somehow pressured her into leaving. Lynda's been acting strange ever since then."

What do I do now? I thought. This would be a perfect opportunity to tell Brad Rick's and my suspicions about what Lynda was doing. But, if he confronted her like Rick thought he would—that could mean real trouble. I had a feeling the injuries Lynda had weren't from a fall at all but from someone who was upset that she had lost a balloon of drugs. I chickened out.

"You're right, Brad. If she's acting differently I wouldn't know. All I've noticed is that she's been busier the last month or so. Maybe what you're noticing is stress from the added work."

"You could be right. I sure don't know. I've offered to help her but she's adamant—she wants to handle that part of the business herself. She tells me I'm busy enough. Which is true, I suppose." He waved his hand at the appointment book. As usual almost all the slots were filled. "Well, I'll have to try and talk to her again." Shoulders slumped, he went back into his office.

CHAPTER 40

▼

Spring had become summer. The sun shone nearly every day and my vegetable garden behind the garage was growing like crazy. I was going to be buried in tomatoes pretty soon. Marmalade was growing rapidly too. The places in her fur where the mats had been cut away were filling in—now I could see the tabby markings clearly. It had taken two rounds of Amoxi-drops to get on top of her respiratory infection, but finally her eyes became clear and bright and her nose stopped running. The ears mites were gone and she ate what Henry and Cleo did. The three of them slept together in a heap most of the time. Brandy became the dog's name after all and she had settled in well. She always had dog food available, but remained rail-thin. This I knew went along with the breed, so I tried not to let it worry me. From her endless energy and lustrous coat I had to assume good health. A quiet dog, she barked only if she felt there was a threat of some sort. I learned to pay attention when she spoke.

Every time I looked at Brandy I was frustrated again at my seeming inability to get any evidence of the drugs I was convinced Lynda was running through her crematory business. I felt like Rick and I were just spinning our wheels. We needed help.

The next morning Henry provided us some traction. He had brought one of his toys into the waiting room and was batting it around the floor when Lynda came in the front door. He jumped up on the counter, leaving his treasure behind.

"I knew it! I knew that damn cat carried that amulet off! Now, where's the rest of it?" Lynda was holding a small circle of blue rubber.

"Isn't that just a rubber band? Henry carries those around all the time and I have to take them away from him before he eats them," I said.

"No, it's not. I can tell. Now, where's the rest of it? It's of no value to you so you might as well give it back." Lynda was leaning over my desk, her face inches from mine. Out of the corner of my eye I could see Henry—his normally pencil-thin tail had puffed up into a bottle brush.

Forcing myself to stay calm, I said, "Lynda, I'm telling you I have no idea what you're talking about. Henry has been playing with that since we got here this morning. I don't know where he got it."

She glared at me for a minute then straightened up. "If you're hiding that amulet you'll live to regret it. And believe me, if you have it I'll find out." She turned on her heel and went to her office, slamming the door behind her. I heard her voice on the phone.

Shaken, I went back to work. Lynda had looked deadly.

Tuesday morning was a bit overcast, it wouldn't be as hot as yesterday. It looked like the perfect day to do some second hand and antique store prowling. I called Georgia.

"So, what do you think? Want to go do some shopping around, maybe hit the stores in Coeur d'Alene and have lunch there?"

Her "sure" was enthusiastic and I headed for town to pick her up.

We shopped all morning, then sat over lunch for over two hours; there was so much we had to catch up on. It was almost dinner time before I headed up the road to my driveway. There was a car parked on the road. That was odd, unless it was broken down that was not a safe place to leave a car. The shoulders were almost nonexistent here. This was a beat-up old wreck, though. Probably did breathe its last here, trying to get up the slight incline. I hoped the owner had called for a tow truck; this would be a real hazard to other drivers once it got dark.

As I pulled into the driveway, I could see Brandy standing on her hind legs with her front paws over the top of the gate looking at me.

CHAPTER 41

▼

Something was not right. Had I forgotten to lock her dog door this morning? As I started to pull into the garage I saw what looked like a flash of light in the living room. Someone was in the house. I jerked the steering wheel to the left and parked behind the garage, out of sight of the house, I hoped. I grabbed my cell phone.

Great. The battery was dead and the cigarette lighter adapter is still packed up with stuff in the house. Now what do I do?

I sat for a minute and pondered. If I tried to drive out again I could be seen, assuming whoever was in my house hadn't already spotted me drive in. My skin prickled with the sensation of somebody watching me. Now is the time to see if Larry's safeguards work, I thought. Maybe I can get into the basement and call for help.

"I can't sit here and just let them get me," I muttered. "Let's do this."

Clutching my keys, I stepped out of the Blazer and pushed the door shut. Keeping as low to the ground as I could, I slipped around to the back corner of the house where the daylight basement sliding doors were. I crouched down under the window sill and reached out for the lock on the fence gate. Then I remembered how rarely this gate got used. I knew the hinges would screech like an insulted mother-in-law. I would have to try and get in through the shop. Hoping the bushes in the back would hide me, I crawled along the fence. Brandy had become fixated on a squirrel in the apple tree—thank goodness that's where her attention was focused. I hoped the squirrel would cooperate and not allow Brandy to spot me.

It was not a particularly warm evening, but by the time I was standing behind the shop, sweat was running down my face. I sent up a silent prayer that the intruders, if they did really exist, were not in there. I slid the key into the lock, took a deep breath, and turned it.

With a tiny snick the door opened. The shop was dim, quiet, and empty. There was just enough light oozing in through the skylights to allow me to see where I was going. I went over to the shelf and felt for the hidden switch. The panel in the floor slid open. I stepped down on the first step and the light came on at the bottom of the stairs. I crept down and hit the switch on the bottom. The panel sighed shut. I was in.

Heart pounding, I went to the bedroom where I had found the security camera controls the day of my first tour. I punched the on switch and a view of my living room came up on the monitor.

"Damn," I whispered. All I saw was the back view of a man, leaving by the front door. I heard him say, "Well, that was a waste of time. Guess we need to get more up close and personal with this bitch." I jumped, I hadn't realized there was audio, too.

I clicked to the other cameras one by one. Except for the bedrooms and bathroom, where I couldn't look, the house was empty and quiet. By the time I switched to the outside cameras they showed me nothing out of the usual. There were no intruders to be seen.

Now what? I knew that activating the cameras would have alerted Sonitrol and they would call the police for me. But my cats were upstairs. I didn't know if I could wait to see if they were okay. I decided to go back out, check and see if the strange car was gone, then go inside.

The shop was as dark and quiet as it had been when I came in. I went out the back door again, but this time walked away from the house and into the woods. There was a deer trail here that led close to the road.

It was getting dark, and I was glad for the cover, but every sound had me gasping, my heart in my throat. It seemed to take forever to get to the road. I just started to peek out of the bushes when the roar of a shotgun flung me to the ground. My eyes squeezed shut, I pressed my face into the dirt.

"Maggie?" I could feel a hand shaking my shoulder, but I could barely hear; my ears rang like the bells at Notre Dame cathedral. It sounded like Sully. I opened my eyes and could just barely see in my peripheral vision the Wellingtons that only Sully wore year round.

"Are you okay? Dang it, I missed them. I seen them guys when they left their car on the road and walked up your driveway. Was they in your house?"

I lifted my head up and looked down the road behind me. The car that had been parked there was gone and Sully stood, legs spread, in the middle of the road. I saw the shotgun in her hand and imagined a faint curl of smoke coming out the barrels.

I spit out dirt and gravel and pushed myself to my feet on legs almost too rubbery to hold me up. "I'm okay, Sully, thank you. Yes, they were inside. I saw them leave out the front when I peeked in the back window." I hated to lie to Sully, after all she was trying to help, but I did not want to tell her about my "Panic Apartment" just yet.

She followed me as I walked down the road and up my driveway. I moved the Blazer back around into the garage then went to the front door. I took a deep breath and pushed my key into the lock.

"You call the cops, Maggie. I'm going to head on home, don't want them to catch me with this gun in my hands; I don't have a hunting license." Sully cackled at me and headed back to her place.

CHAPTER 42

▼

I opened the door to a silent house. Usually when I left Henry home he was waiting for me when I came in. He would have several "kills" for me to exclaim over, things he had pulled off my desk or out of a wastebasket, littered on the floor. He would be sitting amongst them, talking a blue streak. I went looking for him.

He was sitting in his Russian hat pose in the middle of the bed, staring fixedly out the door. I picked him up and instead of wrapping his paws around my neck and purring in my ear, he held himself tense.

"You know we've been invaded, don't you, Henry?" I carried him out to the living room and set him down.

"See? There's nothing out here anymore."

He stood motionless for several minutes then crept across the floor in super slow motion. Belly to the floor, he slid across the living room and into the den. I went in the kitchen.

Obviously, the men I had seen leaving had been searching for something. They had tried to be careful to put things back where they had been, but I could tell, everything just looked different somehow. I knew I had to look around, but I was scared, too. Was anybody still here, hiding in a bedroom or bathroom? I went to the mud room and called Brandy into the house. She wasn't vicious at all, but maybe just her presence would be enough to protect me—she was a big dog, anyway.

Brandy came in and laid down on her pad in the living room. She seemed unworried, but I noticed that the house was still awfully quiet. Cleo always greeted me with glad cries within minutes of my coming in the door, whether I'd been gone eight minutes or eight hours. She would follow me around from room to room, chattering constantly. I needed to find her.

"Cleo, kitty-kitty. Where are you? Cleo?"

I heard a faint meow.

"Cleo?"

"Meow"

"Cleo?"

"Meow."

Back and forth we went. I finally saw her wide, scared eyes peeking out at me from the back of the linen closet.

"Now how did you get in there, you silly thing?" I had to move a stack of towels before I could pull her out. The searchers had been here too. The towels were not stacked the way I had put them away.

Cleo reached out, grabbed me, and hung on. Claws clung to my shirt and her tail was wrapped tight between her legs and across her belly. She looked terrified. I discovered Marmalade behind another stack of towels. She also was rolled up in a tight little ball of terror.

Henry came sliding up to me, whiskers working and eyes dilated to black. Where were the police? I would have thought they would have been here by now.

"I'm calling the cops again," I told Henry.

I reached for the phone and jumped away from it when it rang under my hand.

"Don't be stupid," I said, and picked up the receiver.

"Hello?"

CHAPTER 43

▼

"Maggie, we know you got our stuff," said a raspy, muffled voice. "We checked your house today and didn't find it. You got until eight Tuesday morning to produce it or next time we tear the place apart. Put it in your top desk drawer at the clinic. Understand?"

"But I don't know what you're talking about. Who is this?"

"Doesn't matter who I am, got that? Now, just do as you are told and everything'll be fine, if you're lucky."

With a click the connection was cut. I dropped the phone like it was hot, my hands shaking and sweat starting to ooze down my back. I looked wildly around the room, but all was calm.

The phone rang again. I stood and looked at it. A dancing cobra would be more welcome. The ring seemed to screech at me. Finally, I dried my wet hand and picked the phone back up.

Ms. Jackson? This is Sonitrol. We got the alarm from your house, is everything okay?"

I gulped and clamped my jaw shut for a minute to stop my teeth chattering. "Yes, okay now," I managed to say. "There were two men in my house when I came home and I was able to trigger the alarm…"

"We have called the sheriff," the Sonitrol operator said. "They should have somebody there in a few minutes. Is anybody injured? Do you need EMS?"

"No, no injuries, just scared to death."

"Okay, then. The sheriff should be there soon. Let us know right away if you have any more trouble."

I hung up the phone dropped down into a chair. I needed to talk to Rick, but it took me two tries before I was able to dial his number correctly. I gasped with relief when I heard his voice.

"…and somebody was in here, I saw them leave. I am so scared, can you please come over?"

"Hang on, Maggie, what are you talking about?"

My teeth were chattering again and I had to clench my jaw before I could answer him. "Just come over, okay? I'll explain it to you when you get here."

I grabbed a quilt and curled up in my chair. It seemed like forever, but the clock told me only fifteen minutes had passed with I finally heard Rick's car in the driveway. I let him in and lost the scrap of control I had left. All I could do was bury my face in his chest and cry. Finally I was able to let go of him, sit down and tell him what happened.

"…and I knew for sure they had searched the whole house when all the towel stacks were turned around backwards. They'd been through the kitchen, my bedroom, everywhere. I went to call Marty, but the phone rang before I could. Some guy said I have until Tuesday to return the 'stuff' or they'd be back. Oh, Rick, I'm really scared. What are we going to do?"

"Now we know that it must be drugs, probably cocaine, that's missing," he said. "There wouldn't be that kind of reaction if this really was a missing religious amulet. Tuesday's a ways off. I'm going to do everything I can to get a hold of a box by then. And if I can't, well maybe there's something else we can do. Let's see if we can get set up a meeting with Marty. I have an idea."

"That's great, but what about tonight? I'm almost afraid to stay here. What if those people come back?"

"I don't think they will. They know what they want isn't here. They've given you an ultimatum—I don't think they'll risk getting caught by coming here when you're home. At least not until after eight Tuesday morning. In the meantime, let's call Marty Adams and report this break-in."

I had hoped that Marty would get the call, but he was off duty. Rick left him a message. Finally, two deputies arrived. They told me they were sorry, but they had been tied up with an accident at Argonne and Bigelow Gulch road. They checked the front door and several other surfaces for fingerprints. Both mine and Rick's were on file, Rick's from his service days and mine for my hand gun permit, so they would be able to eliminate us pretty easily, anyway. All I told them was that someone had broken in and I had just seen the back of them from outside as they left. Rick didn't know about the basement apartment and I decided not to tell him about it yet. I told him and the deputies that I had peeked in a back window and saw the burglars leave. I decided that the drug suspicions Rick and I had would stay with Marty for the time being, too. We sat on the couch and watched the deputies work. I would have some cleaning up to do after they were done.

"I hope you're right about whoever it was not coming back," I said after the deputies left. I shivered for a minute. "Rick, this isn't the way I wanted this to happen, but would you stay with me tonight? I would really appreciate it."

He looked at me for a long moment. "Sure, I'll stay. But I'll tell you what. I've wanted to sleep with you for a long time, I think you know that, but not like this. I'll be fine on the couch. We'll save our first night together for a happier time."

Now I was crying again. But these were tears of relief instead of fear. "Thank you so much, Rick, thank you."

The next morning I awoke filled with dread. It was Friday. Rick was gone, but he had let Brandy out and there was a pot of coffee sitting hot in the kitchen, it's fragrance perfuming the air.

I sat down with a cup and looked at the note he had left me. "All was quiet overnight," it read. "I'll see you at work."

I put the note down and wandered out into the living room. I stood and stared out into the yard. Rick and I had until Tuesday to either get Marty the proof he needed or provide a packet of cocaine for drug runners. Talk about being between a rock and a hard place, I thought.

At work I felt like I was being watched constantly, even though nothing was obviously different. The clinic was busy, but time crept. Lunch was a welcome break. I put Henry's leash on him and spent the hour walking him around outside.

When I went back in my mind felt clearer. There was a note in a sealed envelope lying on my desk. I recognized Rick's handwriting: "My place after work" was all it said.

The afternoon passed as agonizingly as the morning had. I was beginning to think life with Phil and his assaultive buddy, Norm, would have been better than this. Even Henry felt the tension—he was sitting by his carrier ready to leave at four o'clock.

Rather than go straight to Rick's, I decided to stop at the Excell Food Store and get us something for dinner. I remembered what the inside of Rick's refrigerator looked like the last time I was there.

Traffic was light. The sky was bruised with black, dark blue, and greenish tinged clouds and I flicked on my headlights as I pulled out onto Trent. A car that pulled out from a side road behind me had one headlight that needed adjusting. The aim was off and it shone annoyingly in my outside mirror. Thank goodness, the car went by as I turned into the store parking lot.

I bought salad ingredients, a package of spaghetti, a jar of Prego sauce and a loaf of French bread. I also got a small can of Friskies for Henry; he'd be hungry too. I loaded everything in the car then turned onto Trent toward Sullivan.

A bright flash caught my eye. There was that light in my mirror again. Could this be the same car? I tried to remember what it had looked like when it passed me on my way into the parking lot but I hadn't really been paying that much attention. This car had all my attention now. I felt the fear of the night before returning. Was I being followed? I decided to find out. I didn't want to lead anybody to Rick's place.

CHAPTER 44

▼

Instead of turning left on Sullivan, I turned right. At the intersection of Sullivan and Sprague there were lots of businesses and traffic. The streets were well-lit too; maybe if I went down that way I could get a glimpse of whoever was on my tail.

The other car didn't stay right behind me, but allowed other cars to get between us. But, the off-aim headlight was like a flashing beacon. It was easy for me to tell it was back there.

I made several stops along Sullivan, Wal-Mart, Fred Meyer, Petco. Each time I left a parking lot the errant headlight went with me. Okay. Now I knew for sure. The next thing I needed to do was shake him off.

Henry was staring out the side of his carrier at me. I could see the fur on his back standing up, he knew we were at risk. Before I left the Fred Meyer parking lot I strapped the carrier in more securely with the seat belt.

I continued south on Sullivan. I remembered Chapman Road that branched off 32nd. I had made a trip out there one day to go to an open house at a Norwegian Fjord horse farm. If there had not been any changes made in the road, it would have several sharp curves in it. One in particular that I remembered might work for me.

I glanced in my rear view mirror. Now there were no cars between me and the car tailing me. The lights from Sprague shone through the car's windows, silhouetting two heads. Great. There were two of them in the car. That was worse. I couldn't let them get me to stop, that I knew.

Sedately I drove south on Sullivan and turned left on 32nd. Keeping my fingers crossed that the road hadn't been improved too much in the years I'd been away, I turned right on Chapman.

So far, so good. The road was still narrow with skimpy shoulders. I increased my speed to fifty-five, ten miles an hour over the limit. The people following me sped up too. I could feel my heart start to pound in my throat. If they decided to ram into me to get me to stop, they would probably succeed. It would be easy to push me off the road into the ditch and there would be nobody to help me. But they stayed a ways back, they seemed to know they couldn't lose me on this road. Chapman Road wound for miles through sparsely-populated land before another county road intersected it.

But, now there were a fair amount of houses along Chapman Road, more than the last time I had been on it. If my followers did decide to try and get me to stop, they might wait until there was less risk of being seen. I remembered that there had been acres of wheat fields at the south end of Chapman. I would have to get away from them before we got that far.

The curve I had in mind was a couple of miles ahead. It was a close to ninety degree left turn beyond a slight rise, followed quickly by another ninety-degree right turn. The pavement stopped just before this second curve too, doubling the hazard. If you were going too fast, or didn't know these tight curves were there, it was easy to slide off the road. I knew, it had almost happened to me. The drainage ditches were deep on both sides. If the car following me slid into one I should have no trouble getting away before they could get back on the road—if they could at all.

My mouth was dry. I tried to relax my hands on the steering wheel and remember all I'd ever heard or read about car racing. Did I spit in my hands or dry them off? They were already sweating, so I guess spitting was out. One at a time I ran them down my pants legs and tried to relax my shoulders. I could see the little rise up ahead. Here goes, I thought, my breath catching in my throat. The pavement under my wheels ended and the gravel road began.

I felt the wheels go up and over the rise. I slammed on the brakes and turned the wheel to the left. I felt the Blazer's rear end sliding off to one side. I released the brakes and floor-boarded the gas. The little SUV straightened out and shot down the road, the two outside wheels nearly in the ditch. But not enough to matter; I was still on the road. I was pleased to see the cloud of dust I had created—that would help too. I knew about an unimproved private road coming up just after the sharp right turn. It looped back across the corner of a wooded field onto Chapman north of the dangerous curves I had just gone through. Hoping the road was still there, I slowed down to look. Yes. There it was.

Once I was in the trees I stopped and turned off my headlights. I rolled the window down and listened. Silence. Okay. I listened to myself breathe for a minute then put the Blazer in four wheel drive and eased the clutch in.

This did not look like it was really any kind of a road, but it was passable. I rolled slowly down what wasn't much more than two parallel ruts, grateful for the remaining light that kept me on the track. Dry branches broke under my wheels sounding like gun shots and I winched with each crack. Could my followers hear me? I tried to ease my death-grip on the steering wheel and concentrate on staying on the path. With relief I found it was cut all the way back through to Chapman Road. As quietly as I could I pulled back out onto the pavement. I stuck my head out the window listened again. Now I could hear what sounded like gravel rattling in wheel wells from tires spinning in the dirt. Someone was shouting. Hoping this was the pair that had followed me, I hurried north down the road away from them.

When I reached the Sullivan-Sprague intersection again I glanced at my watch. I was astonished to see that it had only been an hour since I left the clinic. I watched my mirrors all the way to Rick's. No flashes of a misaligned headlight. Nobody seemed particularly interested in me. When I got to Rick's apartment complex I parked up the street and around the corner. Wishing I had a tarp to toss over the Blazer, I grabbed the sack of groceries and Henry and walked down the street to Rick's place.

"Maggie! I was getting worried. The clinic's been closed for over an hour," he said, opening the door for me.

"Yeah, well, I had an adventure. Here." I handed him the groceries. "Take these in the kitchen. I need a glass of wine, a beer, something. I'll be right back."

I set my purse down and went to the bathroom with Henry in his carrier. I looked at myself in the mirror while I washed my hands. I looked the same, but, oh boy, did I *feel* different. I let Henry out of his carrier and closed the door as I left the room, promising him food soon.

By the time I got to the kitchen Rick had a glass of wine poured for me. I wasn't surprised to see Marty Adams sitting at the table. I'd assumed that's why we were meeting.

I sat down and took a grateful sip. "Well, I'm late for two reasons. I stopped to get us something for dinner then noticed I was being followed. After I made sure I really *was* being followed and wasn't just being paranoid, I shook them off. I didn't want to lead them here."

Both men gaped at me. Marty recovered first. "Did you get a look at the car or the driver?"

"No, not a good one. It looked like there were two people in a light-colored sedan, but that's about it. I led them on a merry chase and they're probably still stuck up on Chapman Road. Maybe you could send a car to find out who they are?"

Marty jumped up and dashed for the phone.

"This whole thing's getting too risky," said Rick. "I think we have to stop."

There was nothing like eluding the bad guys to bolster my courage and my resolve. "No, not now, not when we're starting to get close. Let's talk to Marty and see what he says."

Marty came back. "I sent a car to check out Chapman Road. They'll call and let us know what they find. Now, Rick told me about your house getting searched and the phone call you got. He had an idea and I think it's workable."

"You talk while I cook, okay? High speed chases give me a real appetite," I said, getting up and going to the stove.

"Okay. Here's the deal," Marty said. "If neither of you can come up with anything for me by Monday night I want you to leave this in your desk Tuesday morning like that guy that called you said." He held up what looked like half a blue Bratwurst. "This is filled with cocaine; we'll just have to hope that's what was in the others and that it looks the same, too. We have to leave real stuff—they'll check it before they take it. In the knot at the bottom there's a homing device. We're monitoring it now and will continue to do so as long as it's out of our possession. I don't want either one of you to interfere in any way with this thing once it's in the desk drawer. Maggie, if someone tells you in the middle of the day to go buy a new dress, do it. We'll be watching the building as well as tracking this guy." He waved the blue Bratwurst.

I dished up salad and spaghetti for all of us. We went back over the plan several times. It seemed fool-proof. I hoped it would be.

The deputies Marty had sent to Chapman Road called back. All they had found were signs that a car had slid off the road and been pulled out. "Probably a helpful farmer," they said.

My pursuers were still unknown.

CHAPTER 45

▼

The next morning I woke up to Henry's sneezing. He was back to his old self and was inhaling fingerprint powder from my dresser in the bedroom. I was glad to be able to stay home and clean, the place was a mess. I scrubbed the whole house and threw everything out of the linen closet into the wash, as well as the contents of my dresser. I couldn't bear to think of using towels or wearing clothes that some stranger had handled.

The next day at the clinic things seemed more normal, too. After shaking off that tail, my self-confidence was back. I could tell someone had rifled my desk overnight, but I didn't care. All my handwritten notes were still resting safely overhead on the ceiling tile.

It was lunch time. Brad came and perched on the corner of my desk.

"I tried to talk to Lynda last night about her black eye. She persists in telling me that she fell at the cemetery. I went out there and looked around, but I didn't see any pile of rocks anywhere. I wish I knew what was going on. I've known Lynda since we were both teenagers and in the last year or so she's really changed. She used to always look nice and now…" His voice trailed off.

"I have to confess, Brad, I wondered. You seem to always be so neat and tidy and Lynda, well, isn't."

"Exactly. I don't know if she thinks that because of the work she's doing her appearance doesn't matter or what. But it's not like all her client contact is mail order or on the phone; she still has to meet with people. I don't get it. And, how in the world do you tell someone you don't like the way they look anymore? She denies there's anything wrong, though. I don't know what to do."

I bit my lip. It was all I could do to stop myself from telling him what I thought was going on. But Marty still wasn't satisfied that Brad knew nothing about Lynda's activities beyond what she allowed him to see. I had to keep quiet.

"Have you given any thought to counseling? I know some good folks I could recommend. If not for both of you at least for you—someone you could talk to who might offer some insight?"

Brad rubbed his forehead. "Yes, I've thought about it. Maybe I will have you suggest somebody I could go see."

The telephone interrupted us. It was a client with a colicky horse. Brad grabbed his box of drugs and left.

A burly man in a lumpy suit came in the door as Brad went out the back and got into his truck. "I'm lookin' for Lynda. She here?"

"Let me check—I'm not sure. Your name is…?"

"Tell her Kenny's here."

I clicked the intercom to the back. I could hear noises, Lynda must be working.

"Lynda? There's a man who says his name is Kenny here to see you. Do you want me to bring him back?"

"No," she said, "I'll be right out."

"You been here long? I don't remember you," Kenny said, moving around behind the counter to stand behind me.

"No, I've only worked here for a few months." My insides quivered and I felt the hair stand up on the back of my neck.

His hand brushed my shoulder. "That's what I thought. I'da remembered you and you'da remembered me."

I sat frozen, praying for Lynda to open the door. Out of the corner of my eye I could see Kenny moving closer. I caught a whiff of his sour odor.

"RAUR-RAH-GRRR…PSSSSSSTT!"

"What the hell…" Kenny jumped back.

From under my desk Henry appeared on stiff legs. Every hair on his body stuck straight out. His eyes were wide open, the pupils dilated to black voids. Pulled-back cheeks and an open mouth exposed fangs glistening white against a curled pink tongue. From behind them came a series of growls, hisses, and yowls that would have put a cougar to shame. He jumped up on the counter and I could see unsheathed claws.

By this time Kenny had backed up against the wall as far away from me as he could get.

"Keep that fucking animal away from me," he said, his voice shrill.

Henry was crouched to leap. I went to the counter. "It's okay, Henry. Shhhh, calm down."

"That cat's a menace." Lynda came through the door. "You either control him better or he doesn't come with you any more. Hello, Kenny. Come on back."

Giving Henry a wide berth, Kenny started for the door. He was pale and sweating slightly.

"Henry must have caught an odor of some kind that scared him. He'll be okay now," I said.

Lynda's face was white and sweaty too. She nodded curtly. She and Kenny went into the back of the clinic. When I turned to Henry his fur had smoothed out and he was calmly licking his side.

"Thanks for the rescue, big guy. If that gorilla had touched me I would've thrown up. I wonder who he is? Lynda didn't look thrilled to see him."

I sat back down and tried to concentrate on the payments I had been entering in the computer. Henry jumped off the counter and ran to the door. The UPS man was unloading boxes onto a dolly and bringing them in the door. He moved them to the back of the building, then drove away with a wave.

"If only I could be a fly on the wall back there," I said to Henry, but he just squinted a silent reply to me. I turned back to the computer and saw the intercom on my desk. If I turned it on I'd be able to hear what was going on in the back and what Lynda and Kenny were saying. Maybe I could learn something. Should I take the chance? With Kenny distracting her she might not hear the click when I made the connection. He had been sent to check up on her, I was sure. There was cocaine missing and she was no longer trusted. I would have to be careful though. She'd be able to hear what was happening out front the same as I could hear her.

I switched the phone ringer off. I'd have to watch for a blinking light to tell me if a call was coming in, then talk quietly. Now *I* was pale and sweaty. The radio was on—she might hear it. I reached to turn it off and got an idea.

The computer had come with a microphone. We never used it, it was in my bottom desk drawer. I pulled it out. The plug looked like it was the same size as the tape player/recorder microphone jack on the radio boom box. There were some blank cassette tapes in the desk too. Fumbling slightly, I managed to plug in the microphone and punched "record" on the boom box. I muttered, "testing,

testing","" into it, then rewound and played it back. It worked. I set the microphone as close to the intercom as I could get it and turned it on. I could hear Lynda and Kenny talking. I pushed "record."

The laundry service had delivered a clean supply of towels and cage pads earlier. They were still stacked on the table behind my desk. I took several pads and covered the intercom, microphone and boom box. Then I set the stack of towels in front of the mound I had made.

There. Hopefully any sounds in the waiting room would be muffled and the pile of towels hid my contraption. This also hid the sounds coming from the back. I had to hope the tape recorder was working. Sweating bullets, I tried to get some work done.

Nearly an hour passed and I started to get more nervous. Not only was the tape just a ninety-minute one and I would have to turn it over pretty quick, the afternoon clients would soon start to arrive. I heard a door slam in the back. I reached down and pulled the plug to the intercom. The door opened and Kenny came out, wiping his face, which was an interesting shade of green. Without a word he walked out the front door, got in his car and drove away.

I waited to see if Lynda would be coming out too. She didn't. As quickly and quietly as possible, I disconnected the microphone from the boom box and put it back in my desk. The tape was almost invisible; I left it in the machine. I could retrieve it later.

After switching off the intercom I plugged it back in, then turned it back on. All was silent in the back except for some faint clinking noises. I turned the intercom back off and refolded the pads and carried them into the back and put them in the cupboard. I could hear Lynda rattling things around behind her locked door.

Back at my desk I took the tape out of the boom box and hid it under the pad in the bottom of Henry's carrier. The radio was playing softly and I was busy doing payment entries when Lynda came into the front office.

She was still white around the mouth and I could see sweat rings on her shirt. "I'm done for the day. I think I'll go home."

"You don't look like you feel very good. Are you okay?"

"Yeah," she said, "I'm fine, just tired. Don't forget to lock up and set the alarm when you leave."

"I won't, Lynda. Go home and get some rest. I'll see you day after tomorrow."

"Meow," said Henry, nodding. He was sitting in his carrier with his paws tucked under him. His ample tummy hid the tape's slight bulge.

CHAPTER 46

▼

Rick was unlocking his car. I walked by him and said, "See you later."

I headed up Sullivan Road. There wasn't anybody following me that I could tell. I didn't really care, though, they knew where I lived. On the way I called Rick's house from my cell phone. When his machine picked up I said, "Call Marty."

Rick knew my "see you later" had meant that I would be coming to his house and that he was to go straight there. He also knew to check his machine right away for any further messages.

At home I gulped a container of yogurt then tucked a banana in my purse. The tape went in my pocket. It felt as dangerous as a loaded gun.

I hoped Rick had been able to get a hold of Marty and I was delighted to see his green and white Sheriff's Crown Vic parked up the street from Rick's. As had become a habit, I went on past Rick's apartment building and parked a block away around the corner. I walked down the alley to Rick's back door into his kitchen from his car port. He and Marty were sitting in the kitchen sipping coffee.

"Hi, guys. Rick, you want to pour me some of that coffee? It smells wonderful. And do either of you mind if I finish my dinner?" I brandished my banana.

"No, go ahead," said Marty, "And tell me what this is about."

I took the tape out of my pocket and sat down. "I don't know, maybe nothing. But a tough-looking guy who said his name was Kenny came in the clinic today. He gave me the creeps and Henry didn't like him either—he pulled a wonderful killer-cat routine on him. Not long after this guy arrived and went in the back with Lynda UPS brought four boxes. I turned on the intercom and set up a tape recorder. Hopefully they said something incriminating and also hope-fully, I was able to record it. I haven't had a chance to listen to it yet. Rick, you have a cassette player don't you?"

Rick went to get his tape player. Marty said, "You ought to be a cop. Good work, Maggie."

"Well, we'll see. If I didn't get anything on this tape you'll be changing your mind pretty fast."

Rick started the tape. For a few seconds all we heard were muffled noises and clanking. We all jumped when Kenny's voice blared out.

"You do what you always do and open up all four. I'm going to watch. The boss don't wanta have no shortages this time."

"I've told everybody that one dog only had five last time. There wouldn't be anything I could do with one anyway."

"Except maybe put it up your own nose, bitch. Now get busy."

More random noises. Then we heard Kenny say shakily, "God, that's gross. That smell's makin' me sick." We could hear gagging sounds.

"Here," said Lynda, sounding disgusted, "Stick some of this up your nose."

"Vicks Vapo-Rub? How come?" Kenny's voice was shaking.

"It helps kill the smell. I used to have to use it but don't any more."

For several minutes they didn't speak. Then Lynda said, "Okay, that's the first three and there were six in each. But look, I'm not going to take these out until you see that there's only five in this one. So if anybody's diverting it's not me."

We heard a snorting sound. "Nah, that's right. I gotta list here and one only had five. You're offa the hook for now. Just make sure all twenty-three go out too. I'm gettin' outta here. Any more trouble and I'll be back."

We heard the sound of a door open and close then silence on the tape. "That's when I pulled the plug on the intercom," I said. "Still not much help. They never really say what they're talking about."

Marty shook his head. "No, not really. But, it could give us a place to start asking some questions, that's for sure. We could still use something concrete though. Tomorrow's Thursay. Maybe you'll get a chance to get hold of an outgo-ing box. If not, or if you don't get anything on Monday, leave that blue baggie I gave you and we'll take it from there. Of course, all that gives us is where the drugs end up. Those people won't name Lynda, that's for sure. So..."

"Proof from the clinic would still be the best, then, wouldn't it?" I said.

Marty nodded. "Good luck," he said. He drained his coffee cup and stood to go. "Give me a call."

Marty let himself out of the apartment. Rick and I sat and watched the flames in his gas-log fireplace. The warmth felt good as the day cooled. Without making a conscious decision to do so, I found myself snuggled against his side, his arm around my shoulders. The light coming in the windows dwindled as the summer evening darkened into night.

"Maggie?" whispered Rick.

I turned toward him. He leaned forward and our lips met. A shiver traveled down my back. Deep inside the clenched fist that Phil had left behind loosened, opened and was gone. I felt my lips part, and the tip of Rick's tongue touched mine. He pulled away and looked at me. I nodded.

"Are you sure?" he asked.

Unable to speak, I nodded again.

Coffee. I could smell coffee. For an instant I thought I was home. Henry was a pretty clever guy but I didn't think he could make *coffee.* I opened my eyes and remembered.

I was alone in Rick's bed. My shoes and socks were off, but my clothes seemed undisturbed. What had happened last night, had anything happened? The last thing I could remember was sitting and watching the fire. I shook my head. I give up, I'm going to go and see where that delightful aroma was coming from.

Rick was filling mugs at the kitchen counter. There were boxes of cereal and milk on the table. I could see rumpled blankets and a pillow on the couch in the living room.

"Good morning."

"Morning, Maggie. How'd you sleep?"

"Fabulously, but I'm a little confused. Just what *did* happen last night?"

He grinned. "You mean, did we 'do it'?"

I felt the blood rise in my face. "Well, yeah, that did cross my mind, but I would hope I would remember something like that."

"I would have made sure you did, Maggie. No, you just really conked out on the couch. When you didn't even wake up when I carried you into the bedroom, I decided to let you sleep. We'll have another chance, I'm sure."

"Rick, you are too nice to believe. What time is it, anyway?"

"It's only six, but I thought you would want to be up before I left for work."

"Yes, I do." I sat down and poured Cheerios. "I sure hope we can get something for Marty by Monday. This thing is dragging on forever."

"Shouldn't Lynda be sending out a bunch of urns today? Maybe I'll get lucky and can snag one," Rick said.

"That would be great, wouldn't it? Well, I better get going. I'll see you tomorrow at the clinic." I kissed Rick good-bye and went home.

CHAPTER 47

▼

Cleo and Marmalade met me at the door, Cleo blatting non-stop. Henry sat on the back of the couch with a just-exactly-where-have-you-been-all-night-young-lady? expression. Brandy stood up, stretched and yawned and went to wait for her dog door to be unlocked. I was glad there was always dry food and water out for these guys.

I took a shower and got dressed. Henry was now curled up on the back of the couch and didn't look the least bit interested in having anything to do with me.

"I know, Henry," I told him. "I abandoned you last night, but you'll live. Maybe next time Rick will stay here."

The inside of the fridge was barren and the message light was blinking on my answering machine. I started a grocery list and hit the play button.

"Maggie?" It's your mother." Huh, like I couldn't tell. "Where are you? I just got a letter from Beth and she invited me to come to Ireland and see her. You didn't come at Christmas time and I think you need to come with me so we can all have a nice visit. Please call me when you can."

Wasn't that just like my mother. She is the only person I know who could make a trip to Ireland sound like meeting for lunch at McDonald's. But, much as I would love to see Beth and my niece and nephew and tour Ireland, I still could not afford to go. Besides, I needed to take care of this little drug problem I seemed to be in the middle of.

I dialed her number with fingers crossed. Good. She wasn't home. I left my regrets on her phone and told her I hoped to talk to her soon.

Then I walked around the house, picking things up and putting them down. I needed to do something, but I wasn't sure just what to do. The hobo quilt caught my eye. It just needed a few of the edges clipped before I could wash it and dry it to fluff up the fringe. Maybe this mindless task would give me a chance to think. My brain was in a jumble.

I went out to the studio. It was a bit chilly and I was glad I had the little gas-fired pot bellied stove. I turned on the flames and curled up in my chair with quilt and scissors.

Rick. Did I love him? "Yes, I think I do," I told the room. But was I ready for another serious relationship? After all, I was just starting to be comfortable on my own again. I looked around the studio and thought about the house. Was I ready to share this with someone else? I knew I would not want to move; this was like heaven here in the country with this great quilt shop. But then Rick has never mentioned liking working on his car or anything, and he does seem content in his apartment...maybe he wouldn't want this space for himself...and there is room to build another shop if he wanted one...oh, I don't know. I shook my head, "You're a mess, girl. But, at least you got the fringe clipped."

I tossed the quilt in the washer on a short wash cycle then left it tumbling in the dryer while I went out for groceries.

CHAPTER 48

▼

The world looked different on the drive to work the next day. Colors were brighter, birds sang more sweetly, and even the road seemed smoother. The sight of Rick's car in the clinic parking lot made my heart skip a beat. Funny that *not* sleeping with a man could make me feel like this, but I liked it. Inside the clinic even the cats and dogs looked happy. This I could get used to.

Brad came in at ten. "I was up half the night delivering puppies," he said, yawning. "Lynda had to go see somebody in Bonners Ferry about some cemetery plots and won't be in at all today. She wants you to call UPS and tell them to stop on Monday instead of today. She said she's not quite ready with her shipments."

Rick had come up behind Brad and heard him. He gave me a look over Brad's shoulder, then said, "Good morning, Brad. Hey, I looked at the schedule for this afternoon and we're both are free from two until four. Greg Connors needs the teeth floated on that big thoroughbred of his again. Remember what a circus that was last time? If you could, I'd like you to come along and help me."

"Sure, Rick, I can do that. Let me know when you're ready to go." Brad hung his suede coat on the hook behind the door. I heard his keys jingle in the pocket where he always left them. Rick looked intently at the coat then at me. "Thanks, Brad. I'll holler."

Rick and I both knew Brad wouldn't take a chance on getting his good coat dirty on a farm call—he'd wear his manure-decorated denim jacket. I wasn't surprised when I heard Rick offering to drive—Brad wouldn't need keys at all.

As soon as they were gone I grabbed the key ring. I went to the back and quickly figured out which one would unlock the door to the crematory.

I put the phone on the answering machine and ran to the hardware store. Minutes later I had a copy of the key.

When I got back to the clinic, there was a car in the parking lot. For a minute I was afraid I'd forgotten to write down an appointment and this was an angry client waiting. Then I recognized Stan Watson getting out of his car.

"Brad'll be back in about an hour. Would you like to wait for him?"

"No, that's all right. I don't really need to see him. Just tell him that a body we recovered last week turned out to be that of Sandy Cochran. It looks like she may have been a victim of the same person who's been grabbing women off the street and killing them. As far as I know we got all the information we needed from you last week, but if anything occurs to any of you please call us."

"Oh, no," I said, "That's awful. Does her uncle know?"

"Yes. He's gone back to Michigan and has made arrangements to have her remains sent there for burial." Detective Watson got back into his car. "Be sure and keep us informed if anything comes up."

I watched him drive away then went in and dropped Brad's keys back in his coat pocket. They had barely stopped clinking when he and Rick returned from the farm visit. I had hoped for a chance to get an urn from the back. Now I'd have to wait again.

When Brad and Rick got back and I told them about Sandra's body being found and they looked as shocked as I had been. We talked about it for a few minutes, but none of us had any ideas. By the end of the day Sandra was forgotten.

CHAPTER 49

▼

Rick and I spent the weekend together. It was a glorious time even though we both spent the nights in our own beds. Rick was not pushing me, and after that night at his apartment, I felt a little shy. After all, Rick was the first man in a long time that made me feel happy and I didn't want to jinx it by getting too involved too fast. With the key to Lynda's domain in our possession neither one of us felt any urgency about getting Martin Adams the evidence he needed. Brad was on call Friday night, so we didn't want to risk running into him if we went back after closing time. We decided to wait until the weekend.

Not until Sunday afternoon did we talk again about Lynda, and drugs. We were sitting and reading the paper when I realized Rick was talking.

"I'm sorry, what did you say? There's an article here about Boy Scouts finding a body in Peaceful Valley in town. Sounds like the same thing that Stan Watson told me about the bodies they've been finding. It says someone's been grabbing women off the streets and dumping their bodies in out-of-the-way places. City police have no witnesses and no suspects. I wonder if that's what happened to Sandra. We'll probably never know." I put the paper down. "Okay, tell me."

"I was saying that I think our best bet would be to go in tonight and get one of those urns," said Rick. "We sure as heck won't have a chance tomorrow."

"But won't Lynda know that one's gone?"

"We won't take the whole thing, just the insides. Didn't you tell me you have a camera that'll record the date and time on the film? Bring that. You can take pictures of everything we do and find. We could also take pictures of the shipping labels so Marty will know where to go to find out who's receiving this junk in case there are names that aren't on the disks."

"That sounds like it'll work. How do you want to do this?"

"Let's wait until it's dark and take my car. I'm on call tonight anyway, so if either Lynda or Brad should happen to see it there they won't be suspicious."

We had dinner then curled up to watch a movie until it got dark. Rick made one last check of the answering machine at the clinic. He hung up the phone with a muffled curse. "Sure, *now* there's an emergency call. Let me find out what's up."

He talked for several minutes. I heard him say, "I'll be there as soon as I can, Mrs. Williams. Try to keep her quiet."

"Well, there goes our well-laid plans. Mrs. Williams champion show cat is trying to have kittens and nothing's happening. I need to go see her."

I thought for a minute. "This can still work, Rick. You go see Mrs. Williams and I'll go to the clinic. I can take pictures and get the stuff out of one of the urns without any trouble. You can meet me there after you get done with the cat. If I get done first I'll leave a message on your machine and we can meet back here. What do you think?"

"I hate for you to go there by yourself, Maggie. These are dangerous people."

"I'll take Henry with me. He'll protect me!"

"Oh, right. He's such a killer." Henry was lying limply in Rick's lap.

"He'd be an early warning system anyway. He'll meow or run toward the door if anybody starts to come in. He's better than nothing. I can always say you called me to get you something from the clinic and bring it to Mrs. Williams' house."

"I guess that would be okay. Let's call Marty, too, though." Rick picked up the phone again.

"Well, he wasn't there," Rick said, replacing the receiver. "The best I could do was leave him a message. I better get going. I'll come to the clinic as soon as I can."

He wrapped his arms around me and hugged me tight. "You be careful, now. I'll see you later."

Within just a few minutes I was punching the numbers into the security system at the clinic. The green light came on. Good. The code hadn't been changed. I set Henry's carrier down on the floor by my desk and opened the door. He walked out and started his usual routine.

"I'm going in the back, Henry. I expect to hear from you if anybody comes in, okay?"

"Meow," he said, and bobbed his head.

I headed toward the back. I flicked on the lights as I went. Should Lynda or Brad show up I wanted everything to look like it was on the up and up.

"Now, let's see. If Mrs. Williams' cat was in trouble I'd need to take needles, tubing, a bag of fluids, and maybe an antibiotic, stuff Rick wouldn't have in his bag. I'll put all that together so my story will be believable."

I piled everything I had gathered and put it on my desk. Thank goodness my camera was pocket-size—it wouldn't be noticed.

My copied key opened the door to Lynda's work area without any trouble. Henry zipped into the room ahead of me and started to nose around.

"You're the one who caused all the trouble before, you little stinker. I'd sure like to know where you hid that baggie."

He looked at me unblinkingly for a moment then continued his survey.

Lynda's work table was in the middle of the room. Three boxes on it were ready to be sent out and several more urns were sitting on the table next to their shipping boxes. I opened one. Inside was what looked like a blue bratwurst, remarkably like the one Marty had given me to put in my desk for Tuesday. I started to take pictures.

Once I had a shot of every mailing label, box, urn and blue baggie, I set the camera on the edge of the counter and set the shutter timer. I held an urn and baggie and let the camera take a picture of me holding them. I shoved the camera in my pocket and tried to replace everything the way it had been.

"C'mon, Henry. Let's get out of here." There was no sign of him. "Kitty-kitty, let's *go*."

This is all I need, I thought. "I'm leaving now, Henry. You'll be locked in all night." A sound behind me made me turn. It was Henry carrying a wad of paper. He dropped it on the floor with a faint rustling sound. He looked away from me, his ears swiveling.

"*There* you are, you black devil." I leaned down to pick him up, but he held himself stiffly away from me and stared toward the door. I heard a low growl. Now I heard what he did. Somebody was opening the front door.

"I don't care who's here, Lynda. This will involve the others too, after all Maggie works here and Rick is my partner."

"Brad, please calm down. I can explain everything."

"I hope you can. I couldn't believe it when I saw all that jewelry in the drawer. There's enough there to open a store."

"Well, I knew you'd come unglued about it, so I kept it put away," Lynda said. Her voice sounded like she was sneering at Brad.

"You know that I'd like you to have anything you want, but it has to be gotten honestly. Those receipts were for cash; I know you didn't charge any of it. Where did the money come from, Lynda? The tax returns I sign every quarter tell me that even as much as we're making here there isn't enough coming in to account for that much spending."

"You're right. The pathetic little that this clinic brings in wouldn't buy squat. I deserve nice things and I'm going to have them."

"But the crematory/cemetary part of the business is doing so well and I can only see it doing better. In just a few years the buildings will be paid for then everything will be income. Especially now that Rick is on board and starting to build his client base. There's going to be enough for all of us and we'll be able to move back to Oregon, like we planned."

I could hear the sneer in Lynda's voice again. "Not enough for me. That's why I branched out."

"Into what, Lynda? It can't be anything legal or I'd think you'd have told me about it. So tell me now."

"All right, all right. I'm just doing a job that somebody else would be doing if I didn't. I didn't see why they should make all the money. I saw an opportunity and I took it. All those dogs that come in from Arizona, California, Texas and New Mexico? Each one of them is full of cocaine. I retrieve it, put it in urns and send it off. I make five grand per dog. You know all those urns? After a few expenses for materials and UPS charges, I'm bringing in about $20,000 almost every week. Tax free. Sometimes I do six dogs, that's ten grand more. That's why we're here tonight, so I could show you. C'mon in my office—I don't have any of these records at home. It's easy money, Brad. Easy money."

With Henry struggling under my arm I considered making a dash for the front door. But before I could take a step I heard their voices; they were back in the waiting room. Brad was talking and I could hear shock and outrage in his voice.

"You're selling drugs out of my clinic? My God, what are you thinking?"

"No, Brad, you aren't listening. I'm not *selling* drugs. Merely transporting them."

"But that's just as bad. I can't believe this." Brad's voice was shaking.

"I knew you'd be like this; that's why I didn't tell you. Listen, Brad," she wheedled, "We'll have our future guaranteed. No money worries. I can stop doing this as soon as we've saved up enough. We can go away, travel. We'll be set."

"You really think these people will let you quit? We'd be running from the law and from the druggies," Brad said. "No, this stops now. I'll stand by you, but I'm calling the police."

"That's what you think," she said. I heard a dull thud and a crash. Henry leaped away from me and disappeared behind a cabinet.

Horrified, I turned to the outside door. But it was locked with a key-only dead bolt. The one I had wouldn't open it. I was trapped.

"Maggie, is that you back there?" Lynda called out. "Can you come help me? Brad fell down and I think he hit his head. He's unconscious."

Before I could react the door opened. Lynda stepped through, holding a small silver pistol in her hand.

"Oh, so it is you, Miss Nosy-Parker—just like that Sandra bitch. I'm not surprised to find you snooping around. Oh well, no matter. I can take care of you as quickly as I did her. You being here will actually make it easier. Come on. Get out to the desk and sit down."

"Oh, my God, Lynda, what's with the gun? I'm not snooping, Rick called me and asked me to get him some things. He's with a client and her cat's in trouble. I just needed to find the amoxicillin." I pointed behind me at the refrigerator. Thank goodness I had had a chance to close the crematory door. "Is Brad with you? I thought I heard his voice."

My wide-eyed innocence didn't work.

"Shut up," Lynda said, the gun steady on me, "Do what I said. Get out of here and into the waiting room and sit down at the desk."

Brad was lying on the floor of the waiting room. Lynda had tied his hands behind his back with a leash and bound his ankles together. He looked like he was unconscious, but I could see that he was breathing.

I sat down at my desk. I felt the muzzle of Lynda's pistol against my neck.

"Write what I say," she said, "and make it look good."

I picked up a pen and slid a piece of paper across my desk. I wondered if I dared try to knock the gun away and try to overpower her. But, the muzzle pressure was steady on my neck. She could pull the trigger quicker than I could move.

"Write down just what I say," Lynda said. She started to dictate. I willed my hand to work, my life could depend on it.

'To whom it may concern,

'Brad and I are lovers. He's afraid to ask his wife for a divorce. I can't stand the thought of living without him. If I can't have him she can't either. I hit him in the head and burned up his body, then I took some drugs.

'Now I'll be with Brad in heaven forever.'

"Sign your name. Good. Now, get up and do what I tell you. Stay in front of me."

"This won't work, Lynda. Rick and I figured out what you're doing and we've been talking to the police. Your only choice is to give up. No way is Rick or the policeman we've been talking to going to believe that," I said, pointing to the note.

She chuckled. "I'm sure I'll see Rick tonight. I'll have to arrange a suicide for him, too. And that cop? Piece of cake. Now get moving."

She took me into the back and pushed me into one of the big kennels. She shut the door and fastened the hasp closed with a padlock. I was trapped. I heard Lynda go out to my desk and pick up the phone.

"Hi, Mrs. Williams? This is Lynda at the clinic. Could I speak with Rick, please." There was a pause then I heard her say, "Rick, as soon as you are done at the Williams', please come to the clinic. Brad gave this dog a sedative, so it'll sleep for awhile. But, he needs to do surgery tonight to get the ball out of this dog's gut and he needs you to help. You think it's only going to be about an hour, you say? Okay, I'll tell Brad. Glad those kittens got born quick. Good-bye." I heard her slam the phone down and her footsteps came back to the kennel area.

CHAPTER 50

▼

I was shaking the cage door as hard as I could. Lynda laughed. "Shake it all you want—it won't open. Soon as I tend to Brad you'll be off to la-la land." She laughed again and went to the cupboard on the wall in the adjoining room. I saw her draw up a large syringe of the medication we used to put an animal to sleep for surgery. We had to breathe for the animal with a ventilator; the medication paralyzed all the muscles. A dose that large would kill a human and I knew I was the planned human. Lynda set the full syringe down and went into the crematory.

I sat back in the cage. Now what? I didn't know whether to pray that Rick would come and help me out of this mess or pray that he would stay away and avoid being hurt too. The lovely weekend we had seemed very far away. I couldn't stop my tears.

I could hear Lynda in the back. From the sounds she was making I knew what her plans were—she was going to cremate Brad. The last time she used the crematory was for her drug dogs. His body wouldn't fit until she switched the racks. Maybe Rick would arrive while she was still back there.

"Damn piece of shit!" I heard her yell. "Fucking thing's stuck again. I don't have *time* for this, God damn it!"

I heard more rattling and clanging, but the sounds were fainter. I knew sometimes she had to actually climb inside the chamber to free the rack. Just thinking about it gave me the shivers. I dried my eyes and examined the cage. If I could get out now Brad and I might stand a chance of surviving. I bent my legs up in front of me and pushed on the door as hard as I could. The only result was the wire behind me dug painfully into my back, the cage door did not move. Darn Brad and his secure cages anyway.

The door to the kennel area in front of me opened, making me jump; I hadn't heard anybody come in. For an instant I thought it was Rick. But instead, Henry came through on his hind legs, pushing the door wider with his paws. There was a fat blue balloon in his mouth. He set it down then came over to the cage and stuck his nose through the wire to lick my hand. This made me cry again. Lynda hated him—he'd end up dead too.

"Oh, Henry, *now* you bring me that bag of garbage. You hid it behind that cabinet, huh? I wish you could talk. I'd have you call the cops. I'm sorry, kitty. You've been the best cat ever."

He was only half-listening to me. One ear kept rotating toward the noise Lynda was making. Suddenly he turned and trotted away.

Faintly I heard Lynda. "There, that's got it." Her voice got louder, she was on her way out of the crematory chamber. My time and Brad's was almost up.

"Hey, get away from that you lousy cat. No! Scram. Go away, don't you d…" Clang.

I'd heard that before too. It was the sound of the crematory chamber door closing. There was no way to open the door from the inside—the handle had to be lifted on the outside. Henry had trapped Lynda.

"Yea, Henry! Way to go!" I yelled. Now all I had to do was wait. Rick would be here eventually.

"Help!" The call came from the waiting room.

"Brad. It's Maggie," I shouted. "Lynda locked me in a kennel and I can't get out. Rick will be here eventually. We just have to wait for him. Are you okay?"

"For the moment, I guess. Lynda did what? Where is she?"

"I think Henry managed to lock her in the crematory. She'll be fine until Rick…"

The lights dimmed briefly and I heard a noise that turned my blood to ice water. The crematory was on. Henry must have pushed the start button. Now Lynda was doomed. The high speed burner that had been installed would heat it to 3500 degrees within fifteen minutes. Without the timer set, it would stay at that temperature until somebody shut it down. My stomach heaved at the thought of Lynda trapped inside. What a horrid way to die.

There was a large clock on the wall across from me. If I could get out of this cage quickly enough I might be able to save her. Again I leaned back and kicked at the cage door as hard as I could with both feet. Over and over I hit the door.

The wire bulged out some more, but the door and lock held fast. Exhausted, I finally had to stop. I looked at the clock. Ten minutes had passed. Even if I got out now, by the time I shut the crematory down and it cooled enough to release the heat-controlled door latch it would be too late. Lynda would be dead.

I slumped against the back of the cage and waited for Rick, the crematory oven humming in the background.

CHAPTER 51

▼

Tick, tick, tick. The clock's second hand twitched off each second. I tried not to look at it; when I did time seemed to stand still. Henry came in and sat on the floor next to me. Every few minutes he'd walk to the door and say, "Meow." He was ready to leave and couldn't understand why I wasn't following him.

An hour passed. I was trying to ease my cramped muscles when I heard the front door open and Rick's voice say, "Brad! What the hell happened to you? Where's Maggie?"

The door across from me flew open. "Are you okay? Where's Lynda? Brad isn't making much sense. He said something about the crematory..."

"Rick! I'm all right. Go call 911 then take care of Brad. Henry locked Lynda in the crematory and pushed the start button. It's been over an hour. I'm sure it's too late for her, but..."

Rick was gone.

I leaned my head back against the wire and closed my eyes. I heard Rick go in the back and shut off the crematory. The low hum stopped. He walked by me and went to the phone. I heard him talking to the 911 dispatcher. "Yes, that's right. I have at least one person injured and one that's presumed to be dead. We need an ambulance and police. If you could try and contact Deputy Sheriff Martin Adams...yes...he knows what's been going on. Please hurry, thanks."

Rick came into the cage area with handful of keys. "Let's see if I can get you out of there." He tried several and finally got the door of the cage open. I crawled out and he helped me to my feet.

I clung to him for an instant. "Thank God you're here. Is Brad okay?"

"Yeah, I think so. It looks like he took a pretty good knock on the head, but he knows where he is and what's going on, so I don't think there's any permanent damage. What happened?"

"Not that we need it now, but I got evidence and pictures." I took my camera out of my pocket and pointed to the cocaine-filled balloon on the floor. "Now that it's too late Henry finally brought the bag of coke we thought he had filched from Lynda. I was on my way out when Brad and Lynda came in. It sounded like he had found her jewelry at home and confronted her about how she got it. He was asking her a lot of questions and she finally broke down and told him what she's been doing. As we predicted, he was horrified. When he went to call the police she hit him over the head and tied him up."

Rick led me out to the waiting room and helped me sit down. Brad was lying on the floor with his head on a stack of towels. His eyes were closed but his color was good and his breathing was slow and regular. He looked like he was going to be fine. I could hear sirens coming closer.

"Of course Lynda knew I was here when she saw the Blazer out front. I tried to act innocent and told her that I was picking up stuff for you, but she didn't buy it. She made me come out and write that note." I pointed to my desk. "After she cremated Brad she was going to kill me with a drug overdose; she planned to use one of the anesthesia drugs you and Brad use for surgery, the full syringe is on the shelf in the back by the kennels.

"When I told her you were coming she said she'd arrange a suicide for you too. She had it all figured out. And you know what else? I think Lynda either killed Sandra Cochran herself or helped cause her death. She told me I was a nosy-parker, 'like that Sandra bitch,' and that she'd take care of me like she had her."

Marty Adams came through the front door, gun drawn. "What's going on? What's this about a death?"

"It looks like Lynda was going to kill Maggie and Brad," Rick said. "She…"

"Where is she now? Is she armed?"

"She had a gun, Marty. She was inside the crematory getting it ready to put Brad in when Henry shut the door and locked her in. He pushed the start button. It ran for over an hour." I shuddered. "I'm sure Lynda's dead."

Marty turned to Rick. "Where's this crematory? Can you show me?"

They went toward the back of the building. "There's a bunch of urns full of cocaine back here too," I heard Rick say. The door closed behind them.

The paramedics arrived and on checked Brad. They eased him onto a stretcher and headed out the door.

"Where are you taking him?" I asked.

"Valley Medical Center," they said.

Henry crawled into my lap. He purred, licked my arm and kneaded my legs with his paws. He turned around and around then settled down and went to sleep. I sat and stroked his sleek back. I could hear Marty and Rick in the back. It would be a couple of hours before they could open the door of the crematory chamber and look inside. Because Lynda's body would be removed from the cremation chamber before it could be processed to a final fine ash-like consistency it would be mostly intact, although literally burned to a crisp.

Rick brought a blanket out and draped it over my back. I leaned against the wall and shut my eyes. I wanted nothing more than to go home and crawl into bed with the covers over my head. But, beyond the bare bones of information I had given Marty, the police had not taken a statement. I knew they would want to do that before I left. I tried not to listen to the sounds from the back of the building.

An eternity passed. The county coroner arrived. Lynda's body was recovered from the crematory chamber and taken away. I told my story over and over to police officers of increasing rank. Then a team from the DEA arrived and I had to go through the whole story with them. They questioned Rick by himself then put us together and asked all the same questions again. The interviews were taped. They brought in a camcorder and had us show them everything we had discovered while they followed us, camera whirring. I retrieved my stack of notes from the ceiling and gave them to the investigators, as well as the roll of film from my camera. At last they were satisfied. After telling us not to leave town, and to report to the police station the next day to sign statements, they allowed us to leave.

I was exhausted beyond caring. Rick loaded me and Henry's carrier into his car and took us home. As soon as Rick set the carrier down I opened it and let Henry out. I made sure the dog door was open so that Brandy could get out and that everybody had food and water. I staggered into the bedroom and with my clothes making a path behind me, I headed for bed. I turned off the light and was asleep before the light faded from the room.

CHAPTER 52

▼

An insistent prodding at my cheek woke me up—Henry doing his alarm clock duty with a soft paw. I opened my eyes to see sunshine pouring in through the windows and blue sky. It was going to be a beautiful day.

I started the coffee brewing then got the ad-heavy Sunday Spokesman-Review off the porch. A steaming cup at my elbow, I opened the paper out onto the dining room table. It had been a month since the night at the clinic and it was a relief to see other stories were now headlined.

The investigation was finally over. Marty was coming over for dinner tonight to tell Rick and me the last of the details.

Rick was heavy on my mind again. He was a problem, of sorts. He had made several comments about how he eventually wanted to get married and he'd hinted that he was going to ask me to marry him. I was almost to the point of trusting him, and myself, enough to say yes. I would have loved to find a guarantee that we would always be happy together, but I knew none existed. But, I also knew what I might miss if I didn't take a chance. After facing drug smuggling, threats, attempted murder, and police investigations with him, I felt we could get through anything without losing sight of each other. Phil had been weak—Rick was strong. I heard his knock at the front door and my heart leapt.

Marty pushed himself away from the table. "That was great, Maggie, thanks. Well, are you guys ready to hear the last of it?"

"Yes, please," I said. "Go sit down in the living room and I'll bring dessert and coffee."

Marty took his coffee off the tray and took a sip. "There really isn't a whole lot you don't know. With the information on the disks and the notes you provided, Maggie, plus some more stuff we found in Lynda's office in her computer and with the photos you took, the DEA was able to work both ways and cut off this particular pipeline. There were six people going back and forth across the border into Mexico on a regular basis with dogs. Like you had thought, the dogs were force-fed balloons of cocaine then killed after they were brought back into the U.S. The dogs were sent to Lynda and she removed the drugs and sent them on. She really did cremate the bodies, but we're assuming she just dumped the ashes in the trash. Thanks to you two, we were able to round up some major dealers in Alaska, Colorado, Idaho, Montana and of course here in Washington." He stopped and got up and went to where his jacket was hanging over the back of a chair in the entryway. "The DEA was so grateful for all your help that they petitioned their Office of Rewards on your behalf." He handed Rick and me each an envelope. "I don't know what's in there—I hope it's generous."

I stared with amazement at a check for $25,000. "Yes," I croaked, "Generous would describe it."

Rick's face mirrored mine. He nodded mutely.

"I hope you got something too," I said to Marty.

He grinned. "Yes, I did. You and Rick did most of the work though. Clyde from the Greyhound Park is in jail, too. It turns out that he wasn't an employee of the park, but an independent contractor that supplied them their dogs and also ran the adoption program. Once he realized he was caught he sang like a canary. He was one of the guys who searched your house and threatened you, Maggie. We found his fingerprints in the bathroom. I guess he used your facilities and didn't want to wear his gloves for that. His prints were on the underside of your toilet seat."

Ick. Now I was really glad I had thoroughly cleaned up the day after the break-in.

"You know what else, Marty?" I said, "I actually talked to Clyde one day when he called the clinic looking for Lynda. The day I got Brandy at the Greyhound Park Rick and I made him really nervous. I'm guessing that he recognized my voice."

"Or figured out that we came from the clinic where Lynda did her dirty work," said Rick.

"That's almost a certainty," Marty said. "It turns out that the track only knew about the dogs he bought that they actually raced, not about the ones he sold to the drug runners. Because he didn't kill the dogs himself, the only charge that could be brought against him was profiting from the sale of illegal drugs and an accessory to breaking and entering. His sentence will be short, but at least he's not getting off entirely. Brad, of course, wasn't charged with anything. He'd suffered enough. We found a stash of money hidden in an outbuilding at the pet cemetery which probably went into the rewards. The government decided to let Brad keep the money from the sale of Lynda's jewelry. It's lucky she wasn't wearing it that night.

"Brad told me that he made her take it off after he had found the receipts and insisted she tell him what was going on. She probably had planned for that and had him go to the clinic with her so she could kill him."

I shivered. "She came pretty close to succeeding, too. We have Henry to thank for thwarting her." The feline hero was sound asleep in a basket with Cleo and Marmalade.

"That's about it," Marty went on. "Oh, I talked to Detective Watson from the city police. He said that it ended up that Sandra Cochran died from a Ketamine overdose, that's one of the drugs you use in surgery, right? so they knew she wasn't one of the victims of the serial killer they are looking for. They're thinking she was Lynda's first victim. We'll never know for sure, but we can assume Sandra stumbled onto something and confronted Lynda with it," said Marty. "Now you can update me on what's happening with Brad and the clinic. I noticed you've not been open since that night."

"No, but we've been busy," said Rick. "After all the arrangements were made for Lynda, Brad and I spent the better part of a week together going over the books and discussing arrangements. His eventual goal had been to move to southern Oregon where his family lives and open a clinic/crematory business there. He decided to go ahead and do that now. As we had planned, he's selling me the business. He made me a wonderful deal. It'll be mine in ten years. Maggie is going to stay with me, hopefully for life as well as in the clinic."

Rick got up and left the room. He came back with a catnip mouse. He dropped it into my lap then knelt down in front of me. Taking both my hands in his he said, "Will you do me the honor of becoming my wife?" His eyes were brimming with tears. I felt mine filling, too, and I couldn't speak around the lump in my throat. I nodded. He let go of my hands and picked up the catnip mouse. Around its gray flannel neck was a diamond ring. He slipped it on my finger.

"Meow!" Henry had gotten up and was nodding his head at me.

I took a deep breath. "Thanks for the help again, Henry. Here, I think this is for you." Henry took the mouse into a dim corner where he could roll around on it in private. "Rick, this is beautiful. How did you know what size to get? It fits perfectly!"

"You know how you put your key ring on your finger all the time? I just took that to the jewelers and had them measure it."

"You've missed your calling," said Marty. "You should be a detective."

Startled, I turned toward him. I'd forgotten he was there.

Rick shook his head. "Too dangerous. I'd rather risk getting kicked by a horse or bitten by a dog. Anyway, to go on. Maggie is going to be my assistant. Because she's a nurse she can do a lot of the care for the animals. We're going to hire someone to be the receptionist and bookkeeper. Brad sent letters to all our clients and explained what happened. For the most part their responses have been good. We lost a few, naturally, but we will build back up. We are going to continue with the crematory/cemetery aspect, too. Maggie and I will both be involved with that."

Marty stood up and stretched. "Well, sounds like everything is going to work out for everybody." He shook hands with both of us. "All the best to you two and be sure and invite me to the wedding!"

We walked him to the door and watched until his car disappeared around the bend in the road. Rick turned to me.

"I'm sorry, Maggie. That wasn't really how I'd planned to propose."

"Oh, Rick, it was fine. Marty's practically family. Shall we take a glass of wine out to the hot tub?"

"Sure. Maggie, I love you."

I turned and melted into his arms. "I love you, too."

"Meow," said Henry.

EPILOGUE

▼

Bob O'Reilly was sitting in his supervisor's office. "I'll be Goddamned, oops, sorry, sir," he said. "So, Luis Perez was running drugs. He seemed like such a nice guy, going to visit his mother every weekend. And all those dogs—they were different ones each time?"

The supervisor nodded. "The problem was that they all looked alike. There's no way you or any of the other guys at the other crossing points could have known that he and the others were smuggling drugs. We're going to have to make some changes in the rules for people taking animals across the border, that's for sure.

"Thanks for coming in. We'll let you know what we decide, Bob."

Bob walked out of the office and over to his car. Before opening the door he stopped and stared across the parking lot toward Mexico. Maybe there *isn't* anybody you can trust in this world, he thought.

He shook his head and went home.

THE END

How to make a Hobo Quilt:

You need not know how to make a quilt to make a Hobo Quilt! All you need to know how to do is make a straight seam with your sewing machine. This quilt takes many more words to explain than if I could show you how, but just go step by step and you will see how easily this goes together. If you get stuck, email me your phone number and the best time to get a hold of you. I will call you and we can talk about it.

This is a quilt that each square is made complete, then the squares are assembled into the finished quilt. All you need is fabric, batting, a pair of sharp scissors, and a sewing machine. A rotary cutter, mat, and ruler would make the squares faster to cut out, but scissors will work fine also.

First, decide how big you want your quilt to be, and what size squares you want to use. The larger the square, the fewer you will need to complete your quilt*. For ease of instruction, let's plan on making a single bed or chair quilt 54"x72" out of 6" squares. This means you will need a total of 108 finished squares. Don't panic! That may sound like a lot, but this will go together faster than you can imagine.

Next, decide on a pattern. You can use as many colors and designs for your squares as you like. You can make a crazy quilt, use just two colors in a checkerboard effect, or whatever you like. After the September 11, 2001, terrorist attacks, I saw a Hobo quilt made from all patriotic and red, white, and blue fabrics. It was amazing. I have seen Christmas Hobo quilts too, what fun they are. So, let your imagination run wild.

Fabric: Anything that is not a knit will work, even denim. Flannel makes a soft, fluffy cuddly quilt, but all-cotton ones are great too. You will need enough to cut out enough 7"x7" squares of each color you decide to use. You can figure out your design on graph paper then count how many squares of each color. Most fabric is 44" wide and the salespeople at the fabric store can help you decide how much yardage of each color you will need. For this quilt, you would need to buy 4 yards <u>total</u> of fabric for the top, and 4 yards of one fabric for the back. This can be a plain color or a print, but make sure it goes with the colors, or at least one color in the top pieces, as the back fabric will show on the top. (For example: If you wanted to make a patriotic quilt, don't select green or purple for the back, get red or blue, or a print with red, white, and blue in it.)

You will also need about 3½ or so yards of batting and a couple of spools of thread. I usually use a color that matches the back color, then the quilting does not show so much on the back. The batting can be any thickness and kind you like, thicker battings do cause the pieces of the squares to shift about, so you may need to pin the squares together as you assemble them.

Now that you have all your supplies and know what you pattern is going to be, let's get quilting!

First of all, wash and dry all your fabric (not the batting, unless you are using cotton batting, in that case, follow the pre-shrinkage directions that come with the batt). Iron the fabric smooth, if you need to. This washing and drying step is important to prevent later disasters with uneven shrinking of different fabrics and the possible running of colors.

Then, according to your pattern, cut 7"x7" squares of each color for the top. Then, for this 54"x72" quilt, cut 108 7"x7" squares out of the backing material. The easy way to do this is to cut the fabric into 7" strips and then cut 7" pieces off the strips. You can probably cut at least four pieces of fabric at one time with scissors, and up to eight with a rotary cutter. If using scissors, keep the fabric as flat as possible so the squares will be accurate in size and shape.

Next, cut 108 5"x5" squares of batting. The batting can be cut in strips first too, but beware of trying to cut multiple layers, the batting will slip around.

You can make a paper pattern for the fabric and batting squares and cut around it, if this is easier for you.

To assemble each square: Take a piece of the back fabric and lay it right side down, so you are looking at the wrong side. Center a square of batting on this. On top of the batting place a square of the top fabric, right side up. Sew across this three-layer sandwich diagonally from corner to corner. Then, turn the square around and sew across the other direction. Your stitches should form an "X" across the square. Do this until all squares have been assembled. You can draw a light pencil line across your squares if you need to, or just eyeball it. For a large square, a drawn line is almost a necessity, but anything up to 9" can be done by eye. If your line starts to wander, just wander it back so that it ends up at the corner. A slight variation will not be obvious in the finished quilt. A "walking foot" for your sewing machine is helpful, as the top layer of fabric tends to be pushed ahead by the presser foot (this is especially true for flannel). Or, use three pins, one in the center and one on each side of that one halfway to the corner, to secure the fabric layers together.

To make this process go faster, you can "chain" the squares. This saves both time and thread. To do this: sew diagonally across one square sandwich, then place the next square sandwich in line to sew without clipping the threads or lifting the presser foot any more than is necessary to get the next square started underneath it. Keep doing this until you have sewn across all the three-layer squares. When you get to the last one, just pick up the chain, clip the squares apart and start over on the first one, sewing across the other diagonal to form the X. Then clip the chain apart and your squares are done.

Now is when you need to have your design in front of you, if it is a specific one. Take the first two squares in the first row, working from left to right. Place the BACK SIDES of these two squares together and sew them together, leaving about a ½" seam allowance. Yes, you want the raw edges on the FRONT. Add square 3 to square 2, then 4 to 3, etc. until you have a strip nine squares long. Set this aside.

Repeat this step until you have all 12 strips put together.

Now, take the first strip and with the BACK SIDES together, sew the bottom edge of it to the top edge of the second strip. Repeat this step, bottom edge of strip 2 to the top edge of strip 3, until all the strips are sewn together. Again use a ½" seam allowance. It is helpful to place a pin where the seams in the upper strip match with the seams in the next strip down. This way, if any of the squares are slightly off, you can ease this difference in between seams and won't have one strip longer than the other at the end and all your seams will match. Open out the seam allowances between the squares when stitching strips together to avoid thick wads of fabric at the intersections. This means checking each time to make sure the bottom seam allowance stays in place. This is where I use a pin, both to hold the seams together and to keep that seam allowance in place.

After all the strips are sewn together, run a double line (or if your machine has some sort of setting for a heavy duty stitch use that) around the outside edges of the quilt, about ½" from the raw edge. (An alternative is to make a strip of the backing fabric and one of the fabrics that you used in your squares that is the same width as your squares. Put these strips together with the wrong sides facing each other and sew these along the sides. Do the same along the top and bottom. Run a line of stitching in about 2 inches from the cut edges of the strip all around, then clip in about ½" to make fringe. Make these clips about one ½" apart as directed below.)

The last step is to make the fringe. Carefully snip the raw edges around the outside of the quilt and all the seam allowances that are sticking up on the top of the quilt between the blocks in both directions at about ½" intervals, clipping down toward the seam line. Be careful not to cut through your stitched seam lines.

Once all the border edges and the seam allowances on the top have been clipped, toss the finished quilt into the washing machine. Throw in a two or three large, clean, bath towels with it. Wash on a short cycle with just a little laundry detergent. Then, tumble dry on a permanent press or gentle cycle until dry. Use fabric softener in the rinse cycle or a dryer sheet, if desired.

When the quilt is dry, the snipped seams allowances and edges should be ruffled and raggedy looking. This is how it is supposed to look and the charm of a Hobo quilt. Now, cuddle up and enjoy!

* just remember, decide how big you want your FINISHED squares to be, then cut the fabric 1" larger and use ½" seams allowances for the ruffle. Then cut the batting 1" smaller than the finished square size. For example:

8" finished size squares in quilt, cut 9" squares of fabric and 7" squares of batting. 4" finished size squares in quilt, cut 5" squares of fabric and 3" squares of batting, and so on

If you would like a set of Illustrated instructions for the Hobo Quilt, send $7.50 to cover copies and postage to:

Karen Buck
8804 East Dalton Avenue
Spokane, Washington 99212-2006

About the Author

Karen Buck is a Registered Nurse and professional quilter who lives in Millwood, a small town just outside Spokane, Washington, with her husband, Mike, and son, James Gendron. In between her work as a nurse and a quilter, she finds an occasional moment to write. The Crematory Cat is the first in a planned series of mystery/suspense books featuring Maggie Jackson, nurse and professional quilter and her cat, Henry. You may email Karen at KillerQuilts@aol.com or call her custom quilt company, The Patchwork Heart, at 509 928 8773, with any questions, comments, or suggestions.

0-595-74988-7

Printed in the United States
30627LVS00002B/75

9 780595 749881